LORNA JI

Breakfast *in* HEAVEN

This edition first published in paperback by
Michael Terence Publishing in 2024
www.mtp.agency

ISBN 9781800947887

Michael Terence
Publishing

This book is dedicated to my grand-daughter, Eden.

When Eden was born she transported the light, purpose and sense back into my life at a time when everything seemed dark, despairing and unclear.

Thank you for the joy and love you have given me, my darling.

Granny x

One

Could it be a more perfect morning? It was the beginning of that kind of day when you could write a song, paint a picture, or even climb a mountain. Blue sky, birds singing and the smell of fresh orange juice, coffee and croissants. Oh, if life could always be like this Susa thought, sitting on the balcony of her son's stylish home in an affluent part of town. She loved to sit overlooking the beautiful garden her daughter-in-law Amy so meticulously maintained.

It was the time of year when Susa packed up and went to live at her son's house for a few months. Her little cottage, beautiful as it was, always began to feel a little lonelier as each year went by. Going to see her son and his family was an exciting adventure now that the grandkids, Charlie eight and Martha six, were at the age when they liked to give their exclusive opinions on just about everything. Her role as Grandma had become more important than any of the roles she had played in London's West End. This was real and required more than a year or two of her time. Family was everything to her; she knew only too well how cruel life could be, having had her early years blighted by the taunts and strikes from her abusive father. Never would this sort of behaviour be tolerated again against anyone she knew, if it was in her power to prevent it. That was her promise to herself!

This beautiful morning Martha got up, dressed herself and demanded Gran's full attention. She had become accustomed to the tradition of the endless 'theatre stories' that only Grandma could tell.

"Please Gran, please!" she cried but to no avail.

"Sorry darling, Gran has to dash to see some of her old friends from the theatre this morning. Remember the ones I told you about?"

"But why can't I come?" whimpered Martha.

"You have to go to school. Now go; you and Charlie eat all your breakfast because it's the best meal of the day and makes you strong and healthy. When I get home you and I will have pamper time!"

"Pamper time?" she asked, her voice getting louder with excitement.

"Yes, we'll do our nails and I'll braid your hair," she said, knowing very well that Martha loved having her hair braided.

"Yeah! My Gran's the best!" she chanted, marching around the room.

"Oh, will you stop it, Martha!" interrupted Charlie, casually posing in his cool dark shades in preparation for such high temperatures that weren't forecast for the day.

"Okay, you two, go clean your teeth and grab your schoolbags now!" commanded Amy. They dashed up the stairs. "Are you going to be here for dinner tonight, Susa? I'm making lasagne."

"Oh, I'd love to, but I've arranged to meet Ray at Strings around seven."

"You should have invited him here," replied Amy.

"I would have but he wants to talk to me about something and it seemed important."

Amy sniggered; she had watched Ray and Susa's relationship become much closer these past few years and even made a few comments about it, much to Susa's annoyance.

"Why are you sniggering?" she asked, looking straight at her.

"Now come on, you know. This could be the big proposal!"

"You can't be serious?" she replied, walking slowly to the mirror ad staring back at her reflection.

It was then that Amy realised how genuinely misguided Susa was as to the intentions of her long-time comrade. "You mean you don't think he'll ask you to marry him?" she asked apprehensively.

Susa swung around and met the gaze of the middle-aged brunette, and replied sharply, "No!" She paused for a moment in disbelief "He couldn't! He just couldn't. Why, I could never!" She spoke as if something had awakened within her, something she had allowed to lie dormant from reality for many years.

Shocked, Amy fixed her eyes on the mother-in-law she was beginning to find even more enthralling. "Why ever not?"

"Because I don't love him. Never have. Never will!"

"You don't?"

"No. I could never love anyone the way I loved Owen. Ray couldn't possibly think he was anything more than a friend. It's just so wrong!"

Amy's bewildered look said everything. "But he does, Susa."

"Sorry, Amy, I shouldn't have shouted at you," she hesitated. "It's just I couldn't bear any man to touch me in that way ever again. I can't even bear to think of it." She paused again. "You see a long time ago I had a very bad experience. No one knew anything about it only Owen and my friend Lucinda."

An intrigued Amy moved closer to Susa with an outstretched arm as she could see her eyes fill with tears. "The only time I ever see you cry is when you speak about Peter."

Peter was Susa's brother who had been killed in a road accident when he was sixteen years old. Susa loved him; he was her protector and mentor when she was a child who kept her stable when their drunken father became violent towards her, a well-known character around their village at that time. But this wasn't about Peter, this was about something equally disturbing that her mysterious mother-in-law had evidently buried until now.

"I'm not going to talk about it now. I will tell you that only for Owen I probably wouldn't be here today." From the look in Amy's eyes, Susa realised she had said too much already and immediately changed her tone of speech to a higher, uplifting note. "Ok, that's enough about me. I really am harping on today," she said, nervously fixing the collar of her shirt.

"You know me better than that, Susa. I understand I think, but you can't let anything that happened in your past rob you of your future. You do still have one you know."

Susa kissed Amy on the cheek as the kids came roaring through the door.

"Are you working today, Mum?" asked Charlie.

Amy worked with Ben, a local estate agent, and helped out with the admin when needed.

"Not today love. Now you two go and get into the car and I'll be there in a minute."

They ran off through the garage door from the kitchen to the car.

"I must be off too, I'm parked right in the drive and need to let you out," said Susa as she quickly grabbed her phone and glasses and put them in her large leather bag. She was ready to face the day no matter what.

On the other side of town, Tony stepped off the Virgin Transatlantic flight, trekked over to the car hire reception and received the keys to a very plush black Range Rover. He felt excited about this trip; it would answer a lot of questions for him. He was on a mission to re-unite with family members he had never met. He checked names and entered postcodes into the sat-nav, turned up the music and wound down the windows. He was on his way! His flight had been long, but he'd slept for most of it. Easy when it's business class, he thought!

Two

Amy got into her car and opened the garage door while Susa made her way to a very conspicuous red Audi Cabriolet and slowly moved it out of the driveway, with Amy and the kids not far behind. But as she headed out of the cul-de-sac, she failed to see the Range Rover until it was too late. Tony tried to brake but he couldn't! Susa froze, unable to reverse in case she hit Amy and the kids and just waited for the inevitable crash which happened, sending the car on a 360-degree spin, smashing against the the lamp post, before coming to a halt. Amy could only watch in what seemed like slow motion as the tragedy unfolded and the car settled with the driver's side on the pavement. How could anyone survive this? She thought.

The kids started to scream, "Gran! Gran!"

Panic-stricken Amy jumped out of the car and ran towards the wreckage, but a neighbour grabbed her arm, pulling her back. "No, there's nothing you can do. The ambulance is on its way!"

What seemed like seconds later, the emergency services arrived and had to cut Susa out of the car. It was like a scene from one of Susa's favourite movies. The police made their way over to Amy, who was in shock and trying to calm her distressed children who kept asking if their Gran was dead.

"That's my mother-in-law," she wept, "Susannah Spence. That great lump of a car hit her! Is she going to be alright?"

"We need to get details from you," said the policeman.

"Is she going to be alright?" screamed Amy.

"We don't know at this moment. What's your name?"

"Amy Spence, I'm married to her son. That's my children in the car." At this stage, neighbours headed over to the car to calm the kids down and try to get them back into the house. It was mayhem. Amy gave as much information as she could and caught a glimpse of a very bloody Susa being carefully manoeuvred into the ambulance.

The sound of the sirens disturbed the usually quiet, laid-back neighbourhood. Seconds later, Ben's car sped around the corner, and he jumped out leaving the door wide open. He ran up to Amy and the police shouting,

"What the hell! Where is she?"

"On her way to the hospital now," replied the policeman while Amy grabbed Ben and held him tightly.

"I need to get over there," he said, pushing Amy back and running to his car, then driving off so fast they could hear the tyres screeching down the road.

Another policeman approached Amy. With all the drama, she forgot about the other car and the person involved. "Do you know the man in the other vehicle?" enquired the policeman.

"What?" she asked and looked over at the tall guy climbing into the back of the ambulance. Their eyes hit on each other for just a second. "How would I know him?" she replied confused by the question.

"He has an American accent," replied the policeman.

"So?"

"He seems to know you."

"No, I don't know that murdering scumbag!"

Three

As soon as the ambulance arrived at the hospital, Susa was rushed straight into theatre for emergency surgery. Tony was brought into A&E. The nurse cleaned the deep wound on his face ready for stitches.

"Is the other lady in that car still alive, nurse? Please say yes!"

The nurse could see how distressed he was. "Yes, Tony, she is but she's having emergency surgery."

His face showed his relief. "Like, what just happened, it wasn't meant to be like this. What have I done?"

"Please keep calm down. The police are on the case. They'll find out exactly what happened," she said, trying to reassure him.

"It was the brakes. I couldn't stop. I need to talk to them. I need to see her."

"Let's just get you sorted here. We need to X-ray your arm, just keep holding it like that," she said and fussed about trying to distract him, but to no avail.

Ben was pacing up and down the corridor at A&E trying to piece together everything he had been told about the accident. The day turned to evening before Amy was able to join him.

"How much longer?" a weary Ben pleaded.

They heard the sound of strong footsteps coming down the corridor and the consultant surgeon looked right at him. Ben got to his feet trying to work out from his face if she was dead or alive. He held his breath and Amy grabbed his hand knowing exactly what he was thinking. She tightened her grip the closer the doctor came.

"Are you Ben Spence?"

Ben managed a nervous, "Yes."

"I'm Doctor Carter the surgeon. I was operating on your mother. She has taken quite a blow to her right side and lower back causing renal trauma with damage to her kidney and spleen. There have also been some compressive pelvic injuries and we've had to give her a blood transfusion."

Ben interrupted him, "Is she going to die?"

The doctor paused, cleared his throat and mindfully answered the question, "She's critical at the moment and we've done everything we can at this point. Now we wait. She's in the ICU."

The nurse led them out. Tony had been waiting to see them and made his way towards them calling out, "Ben!"

They turned in surprise. "Who is that?" asked Ben.

A surprised Amy recognised him, "It's that guy who was in the other vehicle."

Ben couldn't hold back and went for him, as Amy grabbed his arm, screaming, "No!"

The nurse shouted for the porter who came straight away.

"Get away from me and my family," said Ben. "My mother could die because of you. I've nothing to say to you, only go back where you came from!"

But Tony begged them to listen while the porter led him out in another direction. "But you don't understand. I need to tell you something. It's important!"

Amy turned to look at Tony and saw the desperation in his eyes. He didn't look like a bad character. Dressed in a designer shirt and dark linen trousers, he had a kind face with a slightly overweight stature. What on earth was so important that he wanted to talk to them about so desperately? And why did the policeman say this man knew them?

They were escorted to ICU and led into a small room, opposite the nurses' station. The soft sound of the pumps of the equipment linked up to Susa had a calming effect as they quietly tip-toed to the two chairs beside the bed. There Susa lay, eyes closed and with scratches on her face. Amy stroked her forehead while Ben sat on the chair closest and held her hand.

"Susa, it's Amy. You had an accident but you're going to be alright I just know it. Ben is here and Charlie and Martha want you back home very soon. Martha's making you a get-well card." Amy went on talking to Susa for a while, hoping to get a reaction, but nothing. She looked at Ben and tears were flowing down his face. Amy put her arms around him and relaxed her head on his shoulder. They stayed in that position for a few minutes until suddenly it dawned on her that no one had contacted Ray. "Oh, no, Ben," she cried. "She was meant to meet Ray tonight."

"Surely someone's told him by now?" he groaned. Ben tolerated Ray for the sake of his mother, knowing they had been good friends most of her life, especially after the death of his father. But Ray's overpowering personality made it difficult for Ben to be around him.

"Do you want me to ring him?" asked Amy.

"Probably better coming from you," he replied wiping his eyes.

She went out into the corridor to ring Ray while Ben sat back down on the chair holding tightly to his mother's hand.

Four

Susa looked so different, barely recognisable, but unknown to Ben and Amy, something strangely supernatural was taking place that they could have no awareness of. With Susa in a coma, she felt herself rise out of her body and glide out through the window opposite her bed. Totally unaware of anything taking place, Ben held her soft limp hand.

Susa's journey took her to a familiar place where she found herself outside a school. She looked around puzzled. Where am I? she thought. What am I doing here? It took a moment or two for her to absorb it all, as she began to recognise her surroundings. It was the old primary school she'd attended as a child. It hadn't changed. A lady came out of the main double doors and walked towards her, holding one of the old hand bells. Why it's Mrs Moss, my old schoolteacher. It couldn't be.

"Can I help you?" she politely asked, and Susa looked around to see who she was speaking to but there was nobody, only her. "Can I help you?" she asked again.

"Are you speaking to me?" she said nervously.

Mrs Moss was a lovely lady in her mid-forties. She had dark, shoulder-length hair pulled back from her face with a large white hairband, and she wore small, round glasses that sat halfway down her nose. Susa caught a bit of her reflection in her shiny specs and saw herself, strangely appropriately dressed for that that era, the sixties.

"Aren't you Mrs Moss, the teacher?" she asked inquisitively.

"I am. What can I do for you?"

"I'm Susannah Spence. Do you remember me?"

Mrs Moss seemed puzzled. She had no idea who she was speaking to and began to look uncomfortable. "I'm sorry, I don't know you."

But Susa answered immediately, "I used to go to this school." And before she got the last word out, she realised how stupid a statement that was.

"You couldn't possibly, this school only opened ten years ago. Are you alright?" She looked at Susa curiously, but it wasn't putting Susa off. After all, you don't often get the chance to go right back in time and she needed to know why.

"Do you know the Henry family from here in the village, Bob and Elsie?" she asked, trying to bring the conversation back to some sort of normality.

"Why, yes, Peter and Susannah attend this school. I'm so sorry I do have to go, it's time for lessons." She walked off and started to ring the bell. All the children ran over to her, apart from a boy who ran down to the back of the playground to a little girl who was dancing quite contentedly on her own. The boy grabbed her by the hand and just like lightning, the thought hit her, was that Peter and… herself? It was, and she felt overwhelmed. She moved closer with her eyes fastened on the two children. Me and Peter, I can't believe it!

Peter ran holding young Susa by the hand while she was telling the teacher, "I'm going to be a famous actress when I grow up, Mrs Moss."

Peter laughed endearingly while Mrs Moss replied, "Even famous actresses need to know their arithmetic, Susannah."

Susa watched as they all went back inside, and she felt stunned by what had just taken place. It had gone very quiet; she looked down at her body and touched the strange purple dress and jacket she was wearing not having any idea where the clothes had come from.

She spied an old Morris Minor car and remembered the rector of the village church drove one of those. This is all bizarre, she thought but was determined to understand why she was there. She walked slowly past some of the shops and the village hall, still in awe of all the old faces she knew as a child, while they looked thoughtfully at this strange woman visiting their village. Then she saw Jonesy's old grocery shop where she spent many pennies on bubble gum and drumstick lollies. She gently opened the door as the little bell rang just above her head and Mr Jonesy suddenly appeared from behind the counter. She walked across the wooden floor to the old man who used to frighten many of the children. But here he was, just a little old man, nothing scary about him.

"I thought you might have been one of those pesky children from that school over there," he said. "You need eyes in the back of your head sometimes. What can I do for you?" He looked at her suspiciously.

"I don't really know. I haven't been in this village for such a long time. I thought I'd just look around." She knew enough to know that Jonesy wasn't just going to leave it at that.

"I remember a time when this was a village. Now they're building here and talking about building new roads up to the city. Whatever next," he said.

"The next thing you know they'll be opening a KFC," she sniggered.

He looked at her strangely and Susa chuckled to herself knowing he hadn't a clue what she was talking about. But that's exactly what did happen to his shop many years later, they made it into a Kentucky Fried Chicken for all those pesky children to go to after school.

"Are you one of the Smiths?" he asked, still staring at her strangely.

"No, I'm not. Sorry, I've got to run. I didn't realise that was the time." She dashed out the door remembering how nosey he was and how all the kids used to call him Nosey Jonesy.

"Huh, city folk," he mumbled.

Five

Susa crossed the road, passed the old telephone box and headed down a lane. She knew exactly where she was going. She couldn't possibly have this chance and not go to her home place. How could she be so nervous when she knew this whole experience was paranormal? She was sure there was a reason for all this and now she had been given the opportunity to find out.

She looked over at the old orchard, saw apples on the trees and thought it must be September. But her heart missed a beat when she spotted the grey van driving up the lane. It was her dad and even though she was a full-grown woman, fear gripped her stomach as those awful memories surged back. Oh, please keep going she thought knowing full well he wouldn't. There were only two cottages down that lane, the Henrys' and Bert and Agnes Smith's.

The van slowed, and the window was rolled down. "Hello there, can I help you? Have you got lost?"

Susa slowly lifted her head and looked right at him. She couldn't speak but she knew she had to. There he was right in front of her, and she had lots of things she wanted to say to him but couldn't. Whatever this journey was about it wasn't about revenge. Her eyes focused on every wrinkle on his forehead, she counted five before she even knew what she was doing, but before she could get to his beady grey eyes, he spoke again,

"Are you alright? Do I know you? You look familiar?"

She threw her shoulders back, smiled and replied, "You must be Mr Henry. I've heard you have really good eggs, so I thought I'd come and find out for myself." She was pleased with that reply. She recited it as well as she would have done in any of her plays.

"Mrs Henry's down the back field," he said. "Give her a shout and she'll come up and sort you out." He drove away slowly, glaring at her in the rear-view mirror.

Susa walked on observing everything. She could now see the home place in the distance, just as she remembered it but then a strange voice startled her, "What do you want around here? I know your name, Susannah Mary Henry."

She turned quickly to see where the voice was coming from. Winston! It was horrible Winston sitting at the side of the lane. He always gave Susa the creeps. Her mum said he was just in her imagination because no one else knew him or had seen him. But there he was once again staring at her with his dark reptilian eyes and ashen face. His small body moved toward her as if in great pain. Feeling intimidated, she moved on quickly and wondered how he still knew her.

A moment later, she arrived at the old broken picket fence that led up a winding path to the little brick cottage with the blue sash windows, home to her for the first thirteen years of her life. Walking down the path she noticed the front door slightly ajar. She carefully entered the hallway and then into the kitchen. It was just as she remembered. The big stove with the kettle on it and the wooden table in the middle of the floor with four wooden chairs that had seen better days. She pulled back the curtain of the pantry where her mum kept all the food and utensils. There was a big box of Sugar Puffs, flour, tins of soups and peas. Not a lot really but enough. No one went hungry even in that household.

This was all so hard to believe but she knew, for some unknown reason, that her time was limited and quickly went up the stairs to her old bedroom. It all seemed so much smaller. Her doll, Primrose, that Aunt Martha had knitted for her was lying on her bed. She treasured that doll. She lifted it and smelt it as she walked over to the window where she saw her mother coming up from the field. She gazed at her in amazement. A tear came to her eye as she watched her mother hunched over, carrying a bucket and wearing her usual green wellington boots and patterned apron that Peter called "Mum's uniform". She looked up for a moment and Susa thought she'd seen her, but she hadn't. Susa noticed for the first time just how pretty her mum was but never did anything about it. Oh, how she wanted to run down those stairs, out back and grab hold of her and hug her. Rescue her from all this gloom. She deserved so much more and so did young Susa.

The door banged and hearing voices, she hid behind the bedroom door. Then came the familiar cry from the young Susa trying to tell her father she was sick and that was why she had got out of school early.

"You're not sick, just acting like you always do. It's all you're good at!" he shouted. "I'm sick too, sick of you pretending."

Those harsh words, so cruel, had affected her whole adult life. She knew only too well how the rejection by her father knocked her confidence, and how those terrible words restricted her for a long time from growing into the woman that she was destined to be.

Small footsteps come running up the stairs and the little girl with pigtails jumped on top of the bed and sobbed uncontrollably into the pillow. There was an argument between Bob and Elsie and Elsie came pounding up the stairs and over to young Susa. She put her hand on her head and stroked her.

"He's just a silly old man. He doesn't even know what he's saying most of the time, pet. Come on now you get into bed with Primrose, and I'll go up to Jonesy's for medicine and sweeties. I won't be long, and don't you worry, Daddy is away to the market and won't be back till late. Peter should be home now too, love."

She tucked the blankets in around her and kissed her. Young Susa's sobs turned to soft whimpers and Elsie left having no idea she had a spectator. Susa made sure Elsie had gone before gently walking over to the bed, sitting down and grasping young Susa's tiny hand.

"You're going to be alright," she whispered.

Young Susa looked up at her and asked so innocently, "Are you an angel?"

"I'm not sure, but one thing I am sure of is you're going to be alright. You have a mother who loves you and a big brother who loves you. And you love your big brother, Peter, don't you?"

"Yes, I do a lot and he helps me with my homework," she replied.

"Don't forget to tell Peter how much you love him. It's important," she answered with tears in her eyes.

"Will you be my friend?" young Susa asked and with such longing it reminded her of how much she yearned for friendship when she was young, to make up for the hatred her father so plainly had for her.

"I am your friend. Now let's go down the stairs and wait for Peter to come in."

Young Susa threw back the blankets and jumped up, excited that she had an angel who knew her and understood her.

"Someday you're going to be a wife, mother and grandmother."

But young Susa was more interested in showing her the little book she had beside her bed. "Look what I have," she said, handing it to Susa, excited for her to look through it. It was The Little Book of Prayers that Aunt Martha had given her. Susa remembered Peter would read one to her each night to help her go to sleep.

They went downstairs together holding hands. Susa touched the textured green wallpaper and looked at the old pictures of world landmarks her mother had hung on the wall. There was the Eiffel Tower, the Taj Mahal and the Hollywood sign, places she knew her mother would have loved to have seen. Then she saw the school photograph of Peter on the table in the hallway. She went over, and just as she picked it up and stared at it, the door opened, and Peter walked in. He saw Susa looking at his photo and asked politely,

"Who are you?"

But before Susa could speak, young Susa replied, "That's my angel."

He laughed, looked again and said, "I know you, don't I?"

Susa couldn't help but stare back at him, astounded that there she was standing with her hero who had taken care of her so well all those years ago. The beautiful brother who showed her that kindness and caring were possible in a hostile and sometimes violent home.

"Peter," she managed to say. "Susa thinks very highly of you." That was the most natural thing she could say.

"Only Peter calls me Susa, but you can too," said the little girl, still holding Susa's hand very tightly.

This divinely appointed opportunity was dwindling quickly. She had little time to do the one thing she regretted not doing, and that was telling him she loved him. Peter moved closer to her not understanding the strange connection. Tears began to run down her face, and she couldn't keep it in any longer. A puzzled but empathetic Peter could only observe Susa's outburst.

"You've been so important to me, and the years I've shared with you have been so precious. I love you so much, Peter. I know you don't understand this. You were the best brother a girl could have. Thank you."

She looked down and young Susa had disappeared. She looked back up at Peter and he smiled at her with tears in his eyes, as if he knew exactly who she was.

"I love you too, Susa," he said. "You'll make it!"

She ran out of the door in tears and heard Winston laughing and mocking.

"I know who you are, Susannah Mary Henry," but before he could get to her, Susa returned suddenly back into her body.

Six

In the hospital room, Amy and Ben were sitting at her bedside. Ben hadn't let go of his mum's hand until suddenly he felt it move and he jumped up.

"She's moving, Amy!" Then he realised she was trying to speak.

"Peter," she whimpered.

Ben moved closer and again, very clearly, heard her say, "Peter."

The nurse came marching in and Ben explained what had just happened.

"Who's Peter?" asked the nurse politely.

"My mother's brother, but he was killed in a road accident many years ago."

"Oh, sometimes this happens. It's like they go back in time," replied the nurse.

"Really?" said Amy. "Seems strange."

The nurse checked to see if everything was alright. "She seems stable," she said. "I'm just outside if you need me."

She went back outside to her desk and Ben felt a bit deflated. He really wanted his mum to wake up and say, 'I'm going to be alright; I'll be out of here in no time.' Sadly not. He settled back in position next to the bed and made himself as comfortable as possible.

"Ray wasn't pleased that I hadn't rung him earlier; I could hear it in his voice," said Amy.

"Oh, who cares?" replied Ben. "The longer we have Mum to ourselves the better, before he comes galloping in organising everyone."

"He won't be over for a while. He said that when he comes, we can both go home and get some rest.

"You see! There he is already organising and he's not even here."

"Ssshhh, come on it makes sense, and we must go home to the children. They need us even more right now," she whispered, trying to keep the conversation calm.

"We'll see," he replied, resting his head down on the bed and clasping Susa's hand.

Meanwhile, another supernatural surge was taking place with Susa. Leaving her body again, she drifted towards the window. She could feel it. How surreal. Where am I going now? she thought. Back to the village and she found herself walking towards the village hall, where she spent a lot of her time with the drama club and any other social event the church held. As she got closer, it seemed something was going on inside. She could hear music from The Osmonds blasting out and some young voices joining in. What on earth? she thought. The Village Hall, I'm back and it's the seventies. Susa knew her pop music when she was young and could pinpoint it to the very year if needed.

She noticed a classic, maroon-coloured sports car pull up outside and a very sophisticated lady got out. She recognised this lady straight away, Mrs Dobson, Lucinda's mum. She elegantly took a cakebox out of the back of her car. She was dressed in a stylish, light blue Laura Ashley smock-frock and knee-high boots. Susa always loved to see her because she looked like a movie star. She was the fashion icon in the village and Susa could see a few peering eyes looking through the shop windows trying to get a peek at the good-looking Mrs Dobson.

"There must be a party or something happening," Susa muttered. She walked over to Mrs Dobson and said hello, but Mrs Dobson didn't seem to notice her. So, she followed her into the hall.

"Oh, Lucinda, turn the music down please or we'll be having Mr Jonesy over with a right telling off!" she shouted and then giggled.

There was her old friend Lu, setting plates and cups down on crisp white tablecloths covering the long wooden tables. Mrs Dobson took the cake out of the box and set it in the middle of the table. "I hope your brother appreciates all this; all the work we've put in to make his eighteenth birthday a special one."

Just then there was a loud noise from the other side of the room. Susa had been so engrossed with Mrs Dobson and Lu that she failed to notice the girl with the long, shiny brown hair trying to lift the tin of crayons she had accidentally knocked over while trying to pin a Happy Eighteenth Birthday poster on the wall.

"Oh Susannah, I forgot you were there!" said a surprised Mrs Dobson.

There she was just thirteen years old and trying so hard not to be awkward in front of Mrs Dobson.

"Oh, Mummy! I don't know what I'd do without Susa," said Lucinda. "She's been a great help."

It dawned on Susa that the night of Darren's birthday party was the night Peter died. Oh No! She watched in horror.

"I forgot the candles. I'll run over to Mr Jonesy's. Be back in a minute," said Mrs Dobson, running straight past Susa and out through the door. Susa wondered why she didn't speak to her. She must have seen her.

"Hello!" Susa shouted and then went over to young Susa but still no reaction. They can't see me, she thought. I wonder why?

Lucinda stopped what she was doing and made her way over to young Susa. "Why didn't you tell Mum? She would understand."

Young Susa stopped what she was doing. "It's too embarrassing, Lu. Oh, why can't my dad be like your dad!" she cried.

The conversation came to an abrupt ending when the shouts of, "Susa, Susa!" came from the doorway and in sprinted a very handsome sixteen-year-old Peter. "It's Dad, he's drinking, and he wants you home but he's really angry Susa, you've got to stay here. Can Susa stay with you tonight, Lu?"

A shocked Lu agreed immediately. "Of course, but that's it, Susa, I'm telling Mum the truth."

At that, Mrs Dobson walked back in. "Tell Mum the truth about what, Lucinda?" she asked suspiciously.

Lucinda told her mum and they all agreed Susa was to stay at the Dobsons'. You could see Mrs Dobson was upset for young Susa as she hugged and reassured her that she'd be alright and that she was never going to let this happen to her again.

I remember her saying that to me, thought Susa, and how safe she made me feel when she hugged me. Oh my, how none of us knew what was about to happen. Susa stared at the stressed Peter who was really trying hard to hold everything together for her. Then Mrs Dobson asked that question,

"Are you going to be alright, Peter?"

"Oh yes," he replied as gallantly as he could.

"No, Peter! You're not! Please stay here, please!" cried Susa just in case there was the remotest chance that she could change this whole tragic event that was about to take place but knowing full well that no one even knew she was there. Peter left. I have to go with him, she thought quickly, after all, I don't know what happened that night and I need to know. I just need to know!

She felt the urge so much that she found herself hastily walking beside him. They passed some of the people arriving at the party. Susa began to talk to Peter knowing full well he couldn't hear but it was like good therapy, updating him on all the undertakings that had taken place since he died. Mum leaving Dad and Dad dying, and Mum going to live with Aunt Martha.

"Oh, Peter, if only you had been there. If only you could hear me. I've so much to tell you."

But Peter kept muttering all the things he was going to say to Bob Henry. They reached the top of the lane and Peter's pace began to speed up, especially as he got closer to the house. They could see their mum, Elsie out in the garden, shouting.

"What is happening?" shouted Peter.

Seven

The sky had darkened, and the drizzle was turning into heavy rain, but this had no effect on Peter. He leapt over the fence and ran to his mum. Elsie had known Bob's violent rages for years now and taken a lot of the abuse herself having become immune to the unloving overtones from her obnoxious and self-centred husband. Tonight, however, seemed gravely worse.

"He's gone mad, Peter. He won't let me in," Elsie cried, getting drenched in the rain.

Susa stood bewildered while Peter looked through the window and shouted, but Bob ignored him and poured himself another glass of whiskey.

"Stand back, Mum, I'm going to kick the door in."

Elsie stood back knowing it wouldn't take much to kick that door in. Peter took a run at the door; his tall gangly form didn't do him any favours, but he managed to break through. They all went in and found Bob in the kitchen with the chair toppled over and broken glass on the floor while he sat on his comfortable chair beside the stove with the bottle of whiskey in his hand. His beady eyes tried to keep up with Elsie as she hurtled around the kitchen, grabbing plastic bags and throwing her belongings into them.

Peter shouted at the top of his voice, "Why are you doing this to Mum?" Susa stood mesmerised by the scene. "That's our mummy and your wife. Susannah is your daughter, and you don't care about her either. What's going on with you? Are you crazy?"

Susa had never heard Peter speak like that before. She was shocked but not as shocked as she was going to be by Bob's reply.

"Yes, I'm crazy!" Bob roared. "Crazy to have taken that whore and her bastard child under my roof!"

He tried to get to his feet but couldn't. There was silence for just a few seconds.

"What?" screamed Susa, "What did he say?"

Peter echoed, "What did you just say? Mum, what's he talking about?"

But Bob butted in, "Go on, Elsie, tell my son about your daughter."

There followed a creepy silence and then Elsie calmly lifted the chair from the floor and sat down on it. She replied in a voice that could only be described as battle-weary but authoritative.

"Bob Henry, you're one of cruellest, most heartless men that ever lived. The only good thing that came from you was Peter Henry and God only knows how someone so caring and generous came from a snake like you. From here on in, you're on your own. I've had enough and you won't treat me or my daughter badly ever again. I detest you!"

Susa had never seen that side of her mother before. At long last, she had stood up to him. He sat there stunned, too drunk to do anything. But what a moment. It made sense now she thought. He was never my father. So, who was?

"You're a stupid, wicked little man. I should never have come back to you. It's the one thing I'll regret for the rest of my life." She didn't care what she said now, it was finished and the one person she held in esteem had found out the secret. The one person she endured years of abuse for just to make sure he was nurtured by a loving mother. It was strange seeing her speak with such emotion. It was like something had suddenly resurrected after being dead for years. Now she had a voice and had made a decision, and it was a decision she stuck by. "And the last thing I want to say to you, Bob Henry, is this; if anyone's a bastard around here it's you! And you know exactly what I'm talking about."

Never was Bob so quiet but it didn't last long.

"But, Mum, what about Susa?" Even Peter's last few words were about protecting her. "I must tell her. She needs to know," he said and ran out frantically.

"No. Peter don't!" shouted Elsie after him but Peter ran on.

Bob finally got the strength and started to run after him, shouting at him for knowing where Susannah was and not telling him. "You're a liar too, like your mother!" he bawled.

Susa glided beside them in this horror show and could barely hear the words of her mother crying, "Peter, come back, I'll sort it. Come back!"

Eight

Peter ran even faster, eager to get Susa to safety and tell her the truth. He hurtled up the lane, the rain now pelting down making vision even harder in the dark, but he could see the lights of the village hall, as he turned the corner. By now Bob was lagging behind but still shouting. Peter then called out to Lucinda, whom he could see, holding a big umbrella to welcome in the guests.

"Lucinda! Lucinda!" he screamed as loudly as he could.

Lucinda heard the shouting amidst the sound of the rain and celebrations. She stepped out in the direction of the voice and saw Peter running up the road, crying out. She immediately shouted for her dad, and everyone turned to look. Her dad and mum come running out. Car lights came up over the hill just before the opening of the lane. Peter looked behind him, not noticing the car lights only the quickening steps of his dad. In a mad dash to rescue Susa, he raced across the road. There was a screech of brakes and then a bang. Peter went down. The few onlookers screamed. Susa stood horrified, watching the aftermath. Bert and Agnes jumped out of the car and ran to their victim. They saw it was Peter. Agnes was screaming and Bert tried to hold Peter, shouting, "No, Peter no!"

They had known Peter all his life as a close neighbour always calling in for a cup of tea and one of Agnes's scones, helping Bert in any way he could and now he lay there on the ground with blood flowing out of him. Both Agnes and Bert knew he was dead. The Dobsons and the others by the hall came running over. The other villagers came out to see what had happened. Just then Bob made it to the scene realising something tragic had happened. He stopped and stood rigid.

"Bob, it's Peter!" screeched Agnes. "He's dead."

Susa watched as Bob ran to Peter and fell to the ground wailing distressfully. There were murmurings from the crowd, "It's Peter Henry, Bob Henry's boy."

Susa could see in the distance young Susa and Lucinda being directed back into the hall. She remembered the vicar's wife and some of the ladies of the church breaking the news to her. How could she ever forget! Little did she know all the things that took place that night, affected her whole life! Yet there it was right in front of her, like having the best seat in the cinema - to watch the saddest movie.

Susa heard someone yell, "There's Elsie!" and turned to see Elsie standing right beside her, petrified. Before she could speak, Muriel Taylor the school dinner lady and the Vicar, Mr Dennis, made their way over to her. The expression on her face turned from fear to great pain after Mr Dennis spoke to her and then he and Muriel had to hold her up while walking her into the village hall. You could hear the sound of the ambulance in the distance. The police constable who lived just down the street went over to Bert and Agnes to try and find out what happened.

Walking through all the commotion and absolute horror, Susa saw her young self, pushing through the crowd and shouting, "Peter! Peter!" in hysterics. Mrs Dobson was behind, trying to hold her back but young Susa was determined. Peter was her rock, and this couldn't possibly be right. He was not dead and how dare people tell such lies? But sadly, she got to the aftermath, and he was now being put on the stretcher with the blanket pulled

over his whole body. She could hear her own s
Dobson put her arm around young Susa and
back into the hall knowing that she had seen
shock made her weak. Susa followed and watche
throwing her arms around her and crying. There were expressions of grief from everyone.

This was too much for Susa. I can't do this again, she thought and went into the very small room at the back where she recalled what happened after that night. She remembered that her mother stayed with Bob until after the funeral. There was very little said and then they went to live at Aunt Martha's. Never again was she to see the resurrected element of her mother standing up for what was right. The price of that tragic event was high. It was plain to see that both Bob and Elsie Henry's lives began to deteriorate after that. Bob let the home place go to wreck and ruin and drank himself to death. Elsie's mental health put a strain on Aunt Martha, though she never complained, and Elsie managed to keep going for a few years after Bob died. She felt that it was her duty to be there for her daughter no matter how she was feeling but began to look at life like it was some kind of punishment. It was all so unnecessary. Why? Why? Why? Those were the days when Susa was so grateful for Aunt Martha's wisdom. She would say, "Susannah Mary, life doesn't always go according to plan, but the good Lord knows all about it and has it all in hand just put your trust in Him. Now you go out and be the best you can at all you can do."

What a lady. She was unique. If only Mum had some of her spirit, her life could have been so different. Martha never married, she just lived to help others and without her inspiration, Susa would never have been the success she was, as the odds were highly stacked against her, except for Aunt Martha!

Suddenly that familiar voice again, "Poor Susa," the taunting sound of Winston. "Sad about Peter"

"What are you doing here?" she answered abruptly.

"Watching and listening," he laughed.

Mr and Mrs Dobson came in. "What are we going to do, Terry?" Mrs Dobson asked her husband while sobbing.

He put his arms around her and held her tightly. "There's not a lot we can do now, love," he replied. "I reckon Susannah would have been so much better off with her real father. Bob Henry's a horrible man and this is all to do with him. That poor girl and poor Peter."

She sobbed on Mr Dobson's shoulder.

"Come on, Tess," he said. "We need to get back out there for the kids."

Mrs Dobson dried her eyes, and they went back out, leaving Susa astounded and shaking her head in disbelief that they had known all the time.

"Everybody knew but you," said Winston, laughing even more deliriously, but before he could say another word, Susa was transported back into her body.

Nine

"I felt her move again!" Ben proclaimed, straightening himself up. "Mum, keep fighting, you're going to be alright."

Susa heard Ben's voice and murmured. Ben drew closer to her, realising she was trying to say something.

"Where am I?"

Ben could barely make her out. "You're in the hospital, Mum. You had an accident," he replied eagerly.

"Need to go back. Daddy," she managed to say breathlessly before falling back into a deep sleep.

"She's going to be alright, I just know it," said Amy, trying to reassure Ben and herself.

"That's a strange thing she said, she needs to go back and then daddy. I wonder what's happening or is she dreaming?" Ben asked. "It's like something is going on that we can't see."

Ben kept talking to his mum, telling her about the kids and about things they were all going to do together when she got better but Susa slept.

Amy began to tell Ben about the conversation she'd had with Susa that morning and about the mystery dinner date Ray had planned for her. Ben was relieved to hear that his mum would never marry Ray. He wondered what had happened to his mum that was so bad.

"I think she was raped, Ben," declared Amy.

"Oh no!" he replied.

"It was the way she looked when she was talking. I've never seen her like that before."

Ben didn't reply, just stared. Amy steered the conversation in another direction, knowing that he wasn't coping well with all the stress. He got up to stretch his legs and a beeping sound came from Susa's heart monitor. The nurse ran in and ordered them to wait in the corridor. The doctor appeared immediately and ordered CPR. Before they knew it, Ben and Amy found themselves sitting in the waiting room.

"Pray, Ben," cried Amy.

"I am."

For the next couple of minutes they didn't speak, just held each other's hands tightly. Thirty minutes went by. Finally, the doctor came out and told them that Susannah was critical and the next twenty-four hours would be crucial. The relief showed on their faces that she was still alive. Then Tony entered.

"What do you want now?" Ben said furiously.

"I just need to know that your mother is alright. I'm so sorry for bothering you, I honestly don't mean to, but I can't leave here until I know she's alright. Please. That vehicle I was driving was hired and I didn't know the brakes were faulty. You can ask the police. Honestly, I didn't know! I'm really sorry."

There was desperation in his eyes and just as the nurse was about to lead him out, Amy stopped her. Ben looked confused.

"Alright, but we need time alone without any hassle, OK?" Amy insisted.

"Yes, of course."

"They've had to resuscitate Susa and we're just going back in to see her now."

Tony's face said it all. He was devastated but his persistence was aggravating Ben.

"My mother's fighting for her life. If you care so much, why don't you leave us alone? If she dies it would be best for you if I never see you again! Do you hear me?" he shouted.

Amy tried to calm him. For some reason, she felt concerned for Tony.

"I'll come back; I have to. I know you don't understand at the moment, but I have to!" he said and walked away leaving Amy baffled by his reply. What don't we understand? she thought. There was more to this she sensed.

Ten

They went back into Susa's room and Ben settled himself into the more comfortable chair that had been upgraded from the last one, while Amy went to get coffee and something to eat. There was no movement at all from Susa, not visibly anyway, but once again, supernaturally she rose from her body and out through the window leading her to another part of her truth-finding journey.

She found herself sitting in the surroundings of the very familiar Ole Playhouse Theatre, where she had performed on many occasions. She looked around feeling like a fish out of water having been more accustomed to performing on the stage than spectating. The lights went down, the music began and the red velvet curtains parted on the play 'Mrs Townsend and Company'. She remembered it well as she had played the leading role. Mrs Townsend was a big hit that ran for a few years in London's West End. That was a busy time for Susa. She received a lot of good publicity from this play as her character was a lot older than Susa, at that time, and she played her with such passion. There was always a standing ovation.

"Oh, my goodness, what am I doing here? Watching myself? It must be the early eighties," she said out loud.

"Sorry, were you talking to me?" said a man's voice.

Susannah turned quickly, shocked that she was heard by the gentleman sitting right beside her. She assumed by the way he was looking at her that she could be seen as well.

"Sorry, no. I was talking to myself," and she nervously laughed.

This was a very handsome, middle-aged man with slick dark hair and moustache along with the subtle aroma of very expensive aftershave. He was gazing at her.

"My name is Patrick, what's yours?" he inquired.

"My name's Susannah," she replied wondering who he was. What if he knew she was from a different time?

"Susannah is a very beautiful name. It was my mother's name, and she was also a very beautiful lady. So, you like coming to the theatre?" he asked.

"Mmm, yes. Well, that is, I used to act on the stage myself," she replied shakily but he didn't notice as he seemed to have become more interested in her.

Why did she have to be plonked beside this man? She just wanted to look around and see if she could spot anyone she had known all those years ago. Maybe he's lonely she thought. Or he could be the reason she was there, but who was he?

Before she knew it, she abruptly asked, "Who are you?" and then apologised for her rudeness.

"Oh, please don't apologise. I'm Patrick Arden. I'm a playwright and I wrote this play."

That shocked Susa. Patrick Arden was a highly acclaimed playwright. He looked different. She remembered him as a kind, retiring gentleman who watched everything quietly from afar, yet here he was chatting away. If only he knew he was talking to his leading lady! She admired all his work. Everyone wanted to work for him and with him but unfortunately, he was someone she tried to forget in her life.

It was at his home, his large country lodge, where she experienced the terrifying ordeal that drove her right to the edge. He had held a party for the whole theatre company and guests. It was at the closing of one of his plays she recalled. Owen had left early as he had to work, and the nightmare began later. Patrick didn't know anything about it but sadly, his name was always a reminder. Maybe that's why I'm here she thought.

"Didn't I meet you before?" she asked. Then thought what a stupid thing to say.

He replied with a large grin, displaying his ultra-white teeth, "Trust me, I would have remembered you. I hope you don't think it's rude of me, but would you like to have a drink with me up in the lounge after the show?" still grinning.

Of course, she had to go. There was more to all this, and he had the answers. "That would be nice, thank you," she replied, smiling back. "What do you think of your leading lady?"

"Oh, she'll go far. I have no doubt."

She looked to the stage and watched the young Susannah Henry give an outstanding performance. She stared as Mrs Townsend cried on hearing the news that her husband had died and remembered how real those tears were, from the years of pain she had been subjected to in her own young life, yet never knowing she too would follow in her footsteps.

An outstanding performance, with a standing ovation and a look of pride from Patrick Arden. He then grabbed her by the hand and led her through the crowd and up a flight of stairs. Susa looked at all the old billboards and posters of some of the shows and plays of that time. There were old photographs of some of the artists who went on to do greater things and make films. She stopped to look at a big picture of herself dressed in the 1920's costume as Mrs Townsend. It was a nice time in her life when she had finally allowed herself to let go of the past and had the support of good friends like Lu and Ray, but also Dr Owen Spence had just made his way into her heart. She smiled at the fond memories.

Eleven

"What would you like to drink?" asked Patrick.

Without thinking, Susa replied, "A latte please." He looked at her confused and she giggled, "Sorry, orange juice."

As Patrick pushed his way through to the bar, Susa had a good look around her. She recognised a voice calling from the doorway and it was Ray wearing the old navy baseball cap he always wore in those days. He shouted,

"Hey, Chip, has Susa come down yet?"

Susa looked over at Chip, who answered, "No, but I've kept a few seats for you over here."

Sad old Chip, she thought, dead and gone. Why did he have to take those drugs? She watched Ray. He was a long and awkward-looking character with a head of brown curly hair. He was one of those men who got better looking with age, but here he was, that funny happy-go-lucky twenty-year-old who idolized the talented Susannah Henry. She watched him intensely as he towered over everyone looking around the busy lounge. She knew he was looking for her. He took over the role of brother for her, always looking out for her even though he would have liked more from their relationship, yet content that he was in even in her life, never wanting to jeopardise that.

Patrick finally made it back with the drinks and apologised profusely for being away so long. Such a kind gentleman Susa thought. It was strange that in all the time she knew him she never had a proper conversation with him. He was always quietly working in the background on the rare occasions she worked with him. She looked to see if he wore a wedding ring but there was none. That seemed sad but she wasn't quite sure why.

"I suppose this brings it all back to you, all the hustle and bustle of the theatre world?"

"Oh yes," she replied, still wondering why she was there. She raised her glass and thanked him.

"It's my pleasure," he said, looking at her in a flirtatious manner.

Susa felt slightly uncomfortable and tried to re-direct him. "It must feel great when you see all these people coming to see your play?" she said, trying to get him chatting.

"I don't think they come for the play but rather the talent of my leading lady," he replied.

Susa was shocked. She wasn't expecting that. She never knew he thought that highly of her. "You think she's that good? Maybe you should tell her?" she said forcefully.

"Oh, I usually keep a back seat with that sort of thing," he said sipping his Jack Daniels and ginger ale.

All these years she never knew this classified information! Would it have made any difference? Yes, it would because his opinion was important in the theatre world. It might just have been exactly what she needed to step into film or TV, or maybe it just wasn't meant to be. Applause rang out, as the leading lady walked in.

"You nailed it tonight, Susa!" shouted Chip.

Susa stared at her young self, making a grand entrance, bowing graciously and looking very confident, but only she knew that this was not the case. And as ever, Ray was faithfully by her side.

"There she is," announced Susa. "Why don't you go over and tell her?"

But he replied solemnly, "My dear Susannah, I don't think she needs any encouragement. Anyway, that awful fellow is with her. There's just something about that guy I don't like." Patrick lifted his empty glass and stood up, asking, "Would you like another?" as he looked over at his leading lady.

"You're a fast drinker, but no thank you."

He went back to the bar, leaving her time to ponder on the statement he had just made. So, she thought, he didn't like Ray. No wonder he didn't make it big in the theatre, she laughed, but still wondered why he had referred to him as an awful fellow. She watched him as he ordered the drinks. He looked all around the bar and then fixed his eyes on young Susa, who was laughing at Ray. He knocked back his Jack Daniels in one go, ordered another and came back to his seat unaware that he had been observed.

"I do apologise, I feel I've neglected you. It's like a madhouse tonight. I would love some of their energy," he said, pouring ginger ale into his glass of Jack Daniels.

"It's their time to be young," replied Susa.

He turned and looked at her. "What a profound thing to say."

Susa laughed and found herself enjoying his company to her surprise. It was clear he felt relaxed in hers even though he was a little intoxicated. He became distracted again and looked over at young Susa. Why was he doing that? she thought, becoming suspicious.

"Why do you keep looking over at Susannah?" she inquired, realising how impertinent that remark was, but also realising she needed to know and wanted to speed things up; time was of the essence.

He took another sip and answered sarcastically, "I do hope you're not jealous. No, sorry, I mean I do hope you are jealous!" and he laughed, putting his arm around her.

"What do you think you're doing?" she snapped. "I think you've had a bit too much to drink," and pulled away.

"Come on now, you're a beautiful woman in the autumn of her life. Maybe you need a little relaxer? How about a Martini?" He looked into her eyes and gave her one of those adoring smiles.

"How dare you! Am I not a little too old for you?" she snapped again, pushing his arm away.

"Whatever makes you say such a thing?" he replied, looking confused.

"You've had your eyes on your leading lady since she came in. She's much too young for you!"

This statement obviously shocked him and he didn't reply at first, then said, "Believe me, Susannah, there is nothing further from my mind. What are you insinuating? She's only a slip of a girl." He looked over again at young Susa and shook his head. "Please forgive my diabolical behaviour. I have so much on my mind at the moment."

She could see he was embarrassed. "I forgive you," she replied and smiled.

"You have such a beautiful smile; I think you are a lovely lady."

Neither of them had noticed young Susa walking past their table. Then she accidentally knocked over Patrick's glass. "Oh, I'm so clumsy. I'm so sorry," she said while trying to wipe it up with a tissue.

"Please don't worry about it. I had nearly finished anyway." He looked particularly nervous, and Susa observed his body language intensely.

"No, I'm going to get you another one," she said. She shouted over to Marty the barman, then got a cloth for the table and ordered the same again. She looked at Susa and asked curiously, "Don't I know you from somewhere?" but Patrick interrupted enthusiastically before she had time to speak.

"Oh, let me introduce you to my friend, Susannah. She is also a fellow thespian."

"You are? My name is Susannah too. Lovely to meet you. Could I buy you a drink as well?" she asked kindly.

"No, thank you," Susa hesitated as she was about to say how she enjoyed the performance but then realised she was talking to herself.

"What have you acted in? I'm sure I've seen you."

Susa tried to direct her attention back to Patrick. "Nothing lately. Do you know this is Patrick Arden, the gentleman who wrote the play you were in tonight?"

This quick action worked, and young Susa turned to him and smiled, "I thought that was you, but I wasn't sure. I've seen you in rehearsals. I'm Susannah Henry."

Patrick looked flushed and nervous. "My dear I know who you are indeed. Thank you for the drink and for making my play very successful."

It was clear that young Susa was happy he had said that. "Your play would have been a success anyway, without me," she said, pointing to her heart. "It gets me every time."

Young Susa left and Patrick watched her go. "What a lovely girl," he said, as if in a trance.

"Why can't you take your eyes off her? I can tell you that she's in love, and he's a handsome doctor who adores her."

Patrick looked bewildered. "How on earth do you know that?" he asked, waiting desperately to hear her reply.

"I have my sources. Are you jealous?"

He looked even more bewildered. "I most certainly am not!"

As soon as he said that Susa asked, "What is it then?"

This was out of character for Susa to be so bold to the point of being rude, but she wasn't going to stop until she found out why he was so fascinated with her young self. Surely, she would have known all those years ago if this older, distinguished gentleman had a crush on her? But never in her wildest dreams did she expect the reply he was about to give her.

"Alright, there is something. Oh dear, I don't even know you. I shouldn't be talking like this."

There was a moment of panic within Susa. What was this something? Her inner being was crying out, but she calmly answered, "Sometimes it's better to talk to strangers. I think you should tell me," she said persuasively.

He looked right into her eyes. "Why do I feel such a connection with you? I feel I could tell you everything. You have such a kind face but with eyes that understand pain. I will tell you."

This was it, what she had been patiently waiting for. What was he going to say? She watched his face change from empathy to guilt and then he said it,

"The leading lady…" he paused and took a deep breath, "is my daughter!"

What did he just say? That can't be right. He's got that wrong! She looked at him in confusion. "What do you mean she's your daughter? She's Susannah Spence?"

He realised how shocked she was. "I shouldn't have said a word. What was I thinking of?" he gasped, putting his hands over his face.

Susa pulled his hands down trying very hard to act like an outsider (her toughest role ever) and give advice. But there he was, her father! There was so much she needed to know.

"Please don't feel that way. I don't know why I reacted like that. Don't be ashamed or embarrassed. If you don't mind me asking, how?"

He paused and stared into his glass. Again, she waited with bated breath wondering how this man could possibly even have known her mother. Never would their paths have crossed. Maybe, just maybe, he'd drunk too much and got this all wrong?

He was about to tell her when Marty the barman came over with a tray of drinks for Patrick and a fruit juice for her. "This is from Susa and the other is from Bill sitting over at the bar."

Patrick immediately waved over to the man sitting on the bar stool, with long greyish hair bunched in a ponytail. Susa recognised him immediately. It was Bandit Bill, the producer. He was a sinister guy and had earned himself a name as a womaniser. Susa never liked him, he gave her the creeps the way he looked at her, back in the day. But that wasn't important right now.

Patrick's reply was, "I wish with all my heart her surname was Arden. Her mother and I became friends-"

Susa butted in sharply, "You knew Elsie?"

He looked at her with surprise. "How do you know her name?" he asked suspiciously.

"I knew of her years back. She was a very quiet lady. It's just I never would have thought of her as your type. So how?"

She nervously laughed with disbelief while Patrick took yet another slug of his drink. Thankfully he didn't acknowledge Susa's strange reaction, but he did want to talk. Little did he know he was speaking to exactly the right person!

"I was staying in the village she lived in doing some research for a play. I met her a few times in the local shop. We got on so well. I would watch for her from the window of the house that I was staying in across from the shop. She was captivating. I never knew anyone so caring and genuine in all my life. She worked so hard on the farm where she lived. We began to meet for walks and sometimes go into the city. We knew we had to be careful because of village gossip and that wouldn't have been fair on Elsie." He stopped and looked at Susa. "That's it!" he said with revelation. "That's who you remind me of. That's why I feel as if I know you. You look like her!" He began to look scared. "Are you related?"

Immediately Susa answered, "No," shaking her head.

He looked relieved and apologised while Susa was trying so hard to hide her overwhelming emotion at everything he was telling her. He was describing an Elsie she had never known. This was intriguing!

He then went on, "I don't have to tell you all the details but for the short time we knew each other we were very much in love. In fact, she's the love of my life." There were tears in his eyes and it was obvious that he had a broken heart. "I was hoping that someday we would meet again. I only just found out that Bob Henry died a good few years back, so I'm going back to the village to see if she still resides there. Maybe we can be together, and we can tell Susannah. Thank you for allowing me to be honest with you." He looked up at Susa; she was sobbing. He grabbed her by the hand. "Oh, what have I done? I'm so sorry. I've made you cry. I'm just a sentimental old fool!"

He pulled a crisp white handkerchief from his pocket and pushed it into her hand. Susa wiped her eyes and managed to pull herself together to reply, "It's not that Patrick, it's just, that Elsie died just over a year ago. I'm so sorry." She could see the pain in his face but trying very hard to hold his emotions together.

"I didn't know," he replied, his mood deflated. "You see I have nobody to inform me of this, nobody knew about the affair, and I promised her I would never discuss it. But I wish now I had as things could have been so different." He put his head down and grabbed Susa by the hand again. "Missed opportunities, Susannah. You can have everything you ever need in life, a nice house, car, money, success, but when there's no love, it's a high price to pay. It just wasn't meant to be my dear. I'm so glad I talked to you, otherwise I would have been going on an empty journey. Another one," he said so quietly.

Susa had watched him as he poured his heart out to her. At long last I know the truth, she thought, even though, up until this point, she never knew she was living a lie. This was her real father and not the cruel Bob Henry she believed was for all those years. She felt a sense of delight as she examined him and focused on his appearance, wearing the whitest shirt she had ever seen and without a crease, just the tiniest accidental splash of Jack Daniels he obviously wasn't aware of. But she also felt his pain and how her existence in this world had turned his life upside down.

Twelve

"It nearly killed me to let another man bring up my child, but I had no choice. I think Bob Henry was unkind to Elsie," he said with such sadness.

"But why did you let her go back to him, Patrick?" Susa blurted out, nearly letting her guard down.

"Because of Peter!" he replied, his voice rising in frustration. "Bob was never going to let Peter go and Elsie couldn't leave him, or Bob for that matter."

"But she did! She did leave Bob right after Peter died!" The atmosphere changed to an air of despair. It was like Susa had taken a knife and struck it through his heart.

"No! I thought she would never leave him. I would have been there for her!" he cried. "I would have married her! I would have given anything to have her and my daughter with me." He couldn't hold back any longer and sobbed.

Susa was completely speechless. This was all too much, then suddenly without even realising, she put her arms around him and held him while he comfortably rested his head on her shoulder. It was hard to comprehend that here she was holding her real father and they were almost the same age. This handsome, kind and loving dad she had yearned for all her life yet never knew he even existed. Her tears also began to flow as she felt all his regret and disappointment release, freeing him from the 'what might have been'. This was Patrick Arden, her real dad, remorseful of the bad choices he had made in life, longing to make amends, but couldn't. If only he knew how much I love him already, she thought, and how I forgive him, her arms tightening around him showing solidarity in the battle of the pain they were both enduring, and it was as if he knew.

It was strange that no one in the bar noticed the scene that was taking place between them. It could be that there was enough drama going on at young Susa's table when Ray suddenly rose to his feet and recited, "Woe unto me for I am a man with unclean lips and I dwell in the midst of people with unclean lips, for my eyes have seen the King!"

And before he could say another word, Chip shouted, "Shakespeare!" and they all laughed.

Then young Susa shouted, "No it's not! It's Isaiah," and she giggled.

Patrick lifted his head from Susa's shoulder and again looked over at young Susa. "Such a bright young lady with the world at her feet. Susannah Mary. That was my mother's name. It was the one thing I asked of Elsie. When the baby was born and if it was a girl to name her after my mother. I'm so glad she did. It makes me feel she's mine when I hear her name being called even though there's nothing I can do about it," he said finishing his drink and banging the glass on the table.

So, I'm named after my grandmother Susa construed. How beautiful. Now she felt like she belonged. It was as if she was a proper person with a heritage. How wonderful it would have been to be able to tell her friends that she was named after her Grandma Arden. All the heartache seemed so unnecessary now and how it all could have been so very different. But she didn't know, she had no idea, and for a reason beyond her wildest dreams, she was given this unique chance to find the truth. There were still many questions.

"Either I've made an utter fool of myself, or you really are an angel. I honestly think both," he said and sighed.

"I know you're no fool, Patrick," she said as he held her hand. "Where have you been since your affair with Elsie?"

He put his hand into the pocket inside his tweed jacket and pulled out a photograph. "Look, that's my other home in the Florida Keys," he said proudly.

Susa stared at it but there was more in that photograph that she needed to know. "How lovely, Florida, but who is that with you?" she asked with intrigue.

"That's my son, Anthony," he replied.

What? He has a son? Suddenly all her wonderful feelings towards him came to an immediate halt. He had a son? But that also meant she had a brother!

"Anthony," she said nervously. "What age is he?"

"He's seventeen."

Susa was speechless and reacted in a more personal way that shocked Patrick. "So, you're telling me that Susannah has a brother she doesn't even know about? Don't you think that's cruel? She has been lied to all these years and knows nothing about this! How would you feel? And how did this all happen?"

Susa was angry and Patrick was confused. "But my dear, the tabloids would have had a field day, and I couldn't do that to her, much as I wanted to, it just wouldn't be fair on Susannah. It would be totally selfish of me!"

Susa was astonished. This man cared more than she could imagine. He had thought it all through sensibly before making a hasty decision. She hadn't thought of it like that, he was willing to make that sacrifice for her and now she could understand. She could feel herself loving him all the more in a deep and tangible way. Oh, how she longed to tell him who she really was.

He went on to explain, "I went to Florida, just for a holiday. I couldn't get Elsie out of my head, and it was affecting my work. It was a close friend who suggested I go away for a while and rest. When I got there, I fell in love with the place, it was just what I needed, and I didn't want to come back. So, I bought a little condo and stayed there. I had a lovely neighbour who became a good friend. She was very kind to me, and one thing led to another. The outcome was Anthony. We never married but I was willing to when I found out she was pregnant. She didn't want to, nor did she want to have the baby. If it hadn't been for me begging her and telling her I would bring him up myself, she would never have had him. So, after he was born, she packed up and left. I wasn't going to lose another child, Susannah! I raised him myself. He's had a good education and is a lovely person even though I do say so myself. I'm very proud of him."

This was a rollercoaster ride of emotions. This time Susa really couldn't speak. She was trying so hard to process all the information she was given. He just gazed at her. It was all too much for them both. But then he asked the big question,

"Why does this affect you so much? We don't even know each other although I honestly feel such a deep connection to you. Why?"

Susa was on the verge of telling him, but something kept stopping her. She knew that nothing could change what had happened in the past. It was done, over, and not even this experience could change it. Maybe this was about the future she pondered, then replied,

"I've had a few things happen to me in my life, Patrick, that are similar to Susannah's, and I too feel a deep connection to you. But I want you to know this, you are a wonderful man, and anyone would be proud to have you as their father. I know that young lady over there would have been so happy to have you in her life. I'm so sorry that it didn't work out with Elsie. Elsie deserved someone as caring and understanding as you. But I have some advice for you, and this is it:

It's never too late to make amends.
It's never too late to forgive.
It's never too late to love and be loved
So, you can allow yourself to live."

He looked at her with tears in his eyes. "Thank you for that."

Susa replied, "My Aunt Martha once told me that. It was at a time in my life when I didn't want to go on living."

Patrick, overflowing with tears managed to reply, "I've really enjoyed your company, but I know I won't see you again."

He took her hands in his and kissed them. This was so emotional; Susa could hardly bear it and she knew that this journey was at a close.

"Who knows, Patrick? I believe anything's possible but not in your foreseeable future. Take care." She got up and walked out of the room, then turned and looked at him but he had his eyes immovably on young Susannah Mary Henry. This time she understood why.

A lot of mistakes had been made and the consequences were painful. But at least she got to find out, and in that, there was a well-spring of healing and an understanding of the madness that enabled her to forgive rather than to regret the misfortunes of choices her parents had made. Then that voice! The one that was becoming all too familiar.

"Susannah Henry! He's a liar! Who do you think you are? You don't know do you!" It was Winston.

"Oh yes, I do. That's my father and you're the liar. Now flee! Out of my way!"

Winston was angry, "Susannah Susa, people are laughing at you!"

Susa disappeared and returned to the hospital room, back into her worldly wounded body.

Thirteen

Ben was sleeping in the chair with his head on the bed, still holding his mother's hand. He felt her move and woke suddenly to hear her groan and then whisper, "Patrick," and again she said, "Patrick."

"Mum, it's Ben. I'm here." There was no response and he turned to Amy, only it wasn't Amy, it was Ray. "Where's Amy?" he asked confused and flustered.

"She wanted to go home to the children, and you were fast asleep, she didn't want to wake you. Maybe we should get the nurse?"

"It's OK, she's been doing this. Who's Patrick?" asks a bedraggled Ben.

"I don't know. Why don't you go home for a while and get something to eat and rest for a while? I'll stay here. It's ten past three in the morning," he said unsympathetically.

"No, not yet but I do need a strong coffee. Mum's been saying daddy quite a bit then Peter and now Patrick. I wonder what's going on?"

Ray looked puzzled. "I have no idea, Ben. All I know is she needs to get through this. I couldn't bear my life without her. I can't believe this. This was going to be such a special night for us."

Ben stared at him in dismay. He didn't want to have this conversation but knew he had no choice in these circumstances.

"I was going to ask her to marry me. We have been so close lately and I just felt this was the right time. I know she would have said yes. Why did this have to happen?" He put his hands up to his face while Ben was left dazed and could only reply,

"I'm so sorry. Would you like a coffee?"

Ben went up to the visitors' room with the coffee machine in it and spied Tony snoring on the chair in the corner.

"No!" he said very quietly and tip-toed over to the machine and put his money in but the noise of the coffee dispensing woke Tony.

"Hi there," he said rubbing his eyes.

"Why are you still here?"

"I need to talk to you, Ben. It's urgent."

He had a nervous look on his face and Ben was too exhausted to argue. "OK, tell me."

"I'm your uncle!"

Ben shook his head in anger. "Will you please go and get your head seen to - you're obviously suffering from concussion - and get out of our lives!"

"No, please listen. I'm Susannah's brother. I only came here for one task and that was to meet the sister I never knew I had until recently and that's your mother. Your grandmother, Elsie and my father had an affair. His name is Patrick Arden. He wrote a lot of the plays your mother acted in." He stopped for breath and looked to see Ben's reaction.

"Patrick? Plays?" This was all a lot to take in. It was surreal.

"Did your mother know? Did she tell you?" asked Tony, with expectation.

"No, nothing, but she said Patrick just now. I know nothing of this," he said getting himself uptight. "This can't be right."

"But it is. That's why I came here. Patrick, my dad is very ill and wants- needs to see her before he dies."

"Right now, she's fighting for her own life, or didn't you know? And why the hell didn't he contact her long ago when she needed him most?" Ben said feeling totally confused with all this information.

"I know! Look I knew nothing about this either until a few weeks ago when my dad was diagnosed with terminal cancer. He wants to explain everything to her. He loved your grandmother, but they couldn't be together because she had a son Peter with Bob Spence."

Ben stood baffled, unable to reply, but also unable to ignore the facts. "OK, go on," he said and looked him in the eye.

"I was on my way to your house when the brakes failed. Your mum was coming out of the drive. I still can't believe this has happened! I was so looking forward to meeting her, and you and your family. This is all a mess, man!" He paced about still traumatised.

This had been a traumatic day, and nothing made any sense to Ben, however, this man seemed genuinely concerned, not psychologically disturbed.

"This is all mad! So, you're my uncle? My mum would love this. She would be so happy about it. She had such a hard life with Bob." Ben went over to the chair and sat down.

"So, he knew Susannah wasn't his daughter?"

"Yes, that's maybe why he gave her such a hard life."

"Not that that's any excuse, man. Dad said he was so happy when she started acting in the theatre. He saw it as an opportunity and wrote plays that your mum acted in. He said she was a great actress and was so proud of her. She was named after my grandmother, Susannah Mary Arden." He became emotional. "I'm so sorry. Maybe this was never meant to be. I just don't know."

He wept while Ben stood in awe. He didn't have the answers. If it was meant to be or not, it was happening, and he had to deal with it.

"Don't get upset. If this is true and I don't have any reason not to believe you, then it changes a lot in our lives. I need to talk to my wife." He went out to the corridor, phoned Amy and told her everything. She was as shocked as him.

"Talk to Ray about it," she said. "He should know about Patrick Arden."

Ray did remember Patrick Arden and even he was amazed by the story. "Susa never knew this. Do you think she needs to know all this now?" he asked, obstinately.

"Why, of course, she does," replied Ben completely flabbergasted by his reply.

"I need to meet this guy! You may be convinced but I'm not so sure. He damn well nearly killed Susa!" He left to find Tony.

Ray had been away for about an hour and Ben started walking a few laps of the room. He'd watched the changeover of nurses many times at the desk outside. Then he heard Ray thanking one of them as he was coming down the corridor. Ben quietly dreaded having his company but wanted to hear the outcome of the discussion he'd had with Tony.

"It all seems to be true. He's gone to his hotel now and he'll be back later," he said wishing he wasn't.

"What do you think?" asked Ben.

"I think he should go home! All too much too late."

"But do you remember Patrick?" asked Ben, carefully.

"Yes, I remember. Drank a lot of Jack Daniels. I never liked him, and I would never have put him and Elsie together that's for sure." He shook his head and looked lovingly at Susa. "This is the last thing Susa needs right now. I wouldn't be happy introducing her to a brother who nearly killed her."

He sat down on the other chair opposite Ben. Ben rolled his eyes too tired to disagree.

"Why don't you go home and get rest and food, Ben? You must be exhausted. I won't leave her I can promise you that."

But Ben was adamant he was staying. He knew that Ray wouldn't leave as he had all the time in the world. Ray was a businessman who had set up his own promotions' agency, called RAW Promotions, his initials being Raymond Alan Whitfield. He had a great reputation, managing many of the showbiz people in the province. He had talked about retiring but never bothered; he hired someone else to run the business so he could take life at a slower pace but still be in control.

They sat quietly together watching over Susa. Ben looked at Ray every now and then thinking over old times. No matter what his feelings were for him, he had always been there for his mum, and him. He was even there when she met Owen after falling on stage and breaking her leg. The 'dashing doctor' she called him, who came to examine her. Ray was heartbroken for Susa when his dad drowned. He was the one who tried to save him, nearly drowning himself in the process. They had all been through so much together. He could understand if his mum did marry him, but thankful she wasn't going to, that was something Ray didn't know, yet. He was irritating though, always having an opinion about everything and wanted everyone to hear it. He began to doze off.

Fourteen

Once again Susa left her body, but she was not daunted this time. She knew there was another piece of her life that she needed answers for, and believed this journey would show her. The all too familiar window led her to a very grand hallway with a sweeping staircase and wood panelling from floor to ceiling. Loud music poured from a very large room with lots of people coming and going. Susa knew exactly where she was and why. She stopped hastily when she heard Owen's name being called. It was him! The handsome man with short fair hair looked totally out of place in his brown corduroy trousers and V-neck sweater. He walked quickly towards the front door. Susa felt her heart beat even faster, just as he'd always made her feel. Owen Spence! She wanted to run over and tell him how much she loved him and needed him, but then realised she was old enough to be his mother. Even though she took pride in her appearance, there was no camouflaging three more decades she was so privileged to have had. Wanting to touch him, she walked hesitantly closer to him, hoping he would catch sight of her first and call out to her, "Susa! My Susa," grab her passionately and they would never part again.

Indeed, he did look at her and said, "Come on now, Susa, you know I have to go."

She stared at him. "You know me!" but a voice came from right behind her saying,

"Owen, please don't go yet!" It was young Susa trying to catch up with him. For a mere moment, young Susa seemed like the intruder who had disturbed this real moment of love and reconciliation, one that had stood the test of time, even though only one remained, an experience unproven to the young Susa. She had to remind herself that this was another supernatural journey with another supernatural purpose, not the ending of a perfect love story. She watched them, wishing that could be her now.

"I'm invisible!" she shouted. No-one heard.

"Oh, just let your hair down for once," said young Susa, longingly to him.

Owen smiled and pulled her close to him. "I have got to go to work but if you want to stay on, I don't mind. You have Lu and Ray here. I know you'll be safe but don't be drinking too much." He kissed her and they went to the door.

"Oh, Owen, please hear me. Don't go again!" Susa whispered, yearning to prolong his company. But the door closed, and he left.

She felt distraught until Patrick bounded down the stairs! It was his party, after all, he was the host. Susa caught him going over to young Susa and she walked closer to hear what was being said.

"Are you alright?" he asked politely.

"Oh yes," she replied. "It's just Owen has to go to work," and she walked off not having any idea who this man really was.

"He's a nice chap, Susannah," said Patrick but young Susa didn't hear him. "I hope you marry him, my darling," he said quietly to himself.

Wow thought Susa. If only I had known that Owen was also leaving me with my real father.

Patrick went back up the stairs following a voice calling him. It was Bandit Bill standing at a doorway. "I set your JD on the table. Why don't you come down to the party, man? I could get you set up with Angie Baby. Come on." That creepy horrible man Susa thought.

"No Bill, you know I'm not one for parties. I just want everyone to enjoy themselves. I know you will anyway," and he laughed, walking into his office and over to a large chair behind a desk.

"You need a hippie cig, man," Bill joked as he left. I'll be keeping an eye on you thought Susa, as he yelled, "Pinky Doll," to some scantily clad woman lingering at the bottom of the stairs.

When he had gone, Patrick came out of the office and went over to the galleried landing where he overlooked the party without anyone knowing. He could see young Susa laughing with Lu. He watched her move about talking to her friends, then he went back into his office and closed the door. She followed him.

He lifted the telephone and dialled a very long number, "Hi, Anthony, it's your dad. I'll be home Thursday. Do you want to go to the game on Saturday?"

Her dad was speaking with her brother. She pondered at how overwhelming this all was; to know now that all this was happening right before her, and she never knew anything about it. But it was time she joined the party. She realised the real reason she was there, and it was nearly that time.

Susa found herself going down the corridor away from the party and entering a room with weird music and a strong smell of marijuana. It was dark, with just a lamp in the corner. There were bodies slouched everywhere and one of them was Bandit Bill watching Pinky Doll dancing provocatively around him. Then she spied Lucinda holding young Susa by the arm and leading her out. This is it she thought. Now I'm going to find out. She monitored the next part of that night with much unease.

"Come on Susa, you need to lie down. I've never seen you like this before. Someone has spiked your drink. I need to get you lying down somewhere to get help," said a very concerned Lucinda and she led young Susa out of the room.

Susa looked around cautiously. She knew what she was looking for. Lucinda led her into a vacant room, where there was a big settee facing a marble fireplace. She carefully lay Susa down, took a tartan blanket that was draped over a chair and wrapped it around her. Then she brought the gold coal bucket from the hearth and placed it beside her.

"That's if you need to be sick, Susa. I'm going to get you water and help. I won't be long."

Lu ran out quickly. Susa watched frantically, remembering how sick she had felt. Suddenly the lights went out. There were voices of panic and some laughter. Fortunately, bright moonlight filtered through the large window. Then the door opened, and a hooded figure came into the room.

"Oh no!" she cried as she heard young Susa whimper, "Who are you, scumbag?" She screamed but couldn't see who it was. The figure lay across young Susa, panting, and young Susa was unable to cry out for help.

"Damn it, it's you, Bill, I know it's you!" The ordeal was over in minutes and the cloaked figure ran out.

Susa followed; this was her opportunity to know once and for all who had raped her. All her life she had kept this a closely guarded secret. Now she would find out who the perpetrator was.

The lights came back on, and she found herself in a small room where all the electrics were, and the hooded figure! The tall figure quickly took off his cloak, not realising he had company. He turned right around in perfect sight of Susa.

"Ray!" she cried out in shock.

He quickly stuffed the cloak into a cloth bag and hid it behind a box. Then he opened the door and shouted, "I fixed it!" like he was the hero who saved the day.

Susa was in turmoil, her mind questioning everything. How did I not know? she cried. How did he fool me all those years? Am I so blind and stupid? Her stomach churned thinking of how all these years she fondly cared for him, and he was her rapist! This was too much! Is there nothing in my life that's true? she sobbed while she watched the aftermath.

Patrick came running up the corridor to Ray shouting, "What did you do? Why are you in there?"

"I got the lights back on, Mr Arden," Ray said so reassuringly, but Patrick wasn't convinced.

"It's not who switched them on I care about but who switched them off, and why?" he demanded.

"Oh, I don't know who switched them off, Mr Arden," he replied confidently.

Patrick closed the door and made everyone go up to the top end of the house where the party was continuing, none of them aware of what had just taken place. Lucinda called Ray and he turned quickly and walked towards her.

"What?"

"It's Susa, someone has spiked her drink!" she shouted. "Follow me, she's in this room, down here."

They walked in and Ray played a blinder, the best acting he ever did in his role as the caring, concerned friend. Susa was lying lifeless on the settee groaning and sweating.

"Oh, Susa! What's happened you?" he said, running to her and pretending to be upset. Patrick followed them.

"What happened here, Lucinda?"

"Someone spiked her drink. She can't talk but it's like she's trying to tell me something and I don't know what it is," she replied with tears running down her face. "I'm sorry."

Lucinda seemed very nervous. Patrick walked over to Ray and looked him right in the eye. "Go and phone an ambulance and then phone Owen. Do you hear me? Now!" he shouted, angrily.

Ray obediently dashed out. Lucinda sat down beside young Susa and held her hand while Patrick looked around the room in deep thought. "I thought this would have been the safest place in the world for Susannah," he said. "Who did this to her?" He knelt down beside her on the floor and rested his hand on her face in a caring, compassionate way. "Go to the bathroom next door quickly, Lucinda, and get water and a damp face cloth." Lucinda rushed off immediately. "Oh, Susannah," he continued, "I'm so sorry. Please get that Ray fellow out of your life. I don't trust him. He'll never make it in acting, I'll make damn sure of that."

An astonished Susa watched as Ray came back in and told Patrick that the ambulance was on its way and that Owen had been contacted. Just as Ray tried to make his way over to Susa, Patrick stopped him and asked him to leave. "The people that need to be here are here. You can go."

Ray looked at him furiously but said nothing and marched out. Lu came back in and gave Susa some water on her lips and wiped her forehead with a wet cloth.

"Please look after her, Lucinda and ring me. Let me know she's alright?"

"I will, of course, Mr Arden," she replied.

Did Lucinda know that Patrick was her father? She certainly didn't seem too shocked at how concerned Patrick was about all of this. Lu never told me she'd rung him, or even that he had asked her to, she thought. One thing was for sure, Patrick Arden had Ray sussed. He never liked him. Good old Daddy, she thought, even though her heart was breaking with the knowledge that this lovely man, with all the wisdom and compassion a daughter needed, yearned to be at the very least a good host in her life, and even that was a disaster. What a mess! Young Susa was taken out on a stretcher by the medics while Patrick and Lu followed. She knew all too well the trauma that followed the next few years, yet her friendship with Lucinda became stronger and her relationship with Owen blossomed, even though that dreadful night had certainly challenged it.

It was time to go back into her mortal body. The room darkened then she heard the laughter and turned to see Winston sitting on the ornate red and gold chair over in the corner. "You think you know everything, Susannah Mary," he stuttered. "Don't you?" He wriggled off the chair and hobbled over to her dragging his feet looking dark and disfigured.

Susa glared at him, all the fear she had for him had gone. "You wanna know what I think?" she asked, smiling. "I think you're scared of me because the more I get to know the truth, the smaller and more hideous you become," and she laughed. He was furious trying to grab her but couldn't. "See, you have no power. Now go to hell where you belong!"

The room seemed to get darker and smaller and then he shouted, "But you don't know everything. There's something else," and he began to laugh in his hysterical way. "It was your new brother Anthony who hit your car. So, your new family isn't that great either. Poor Susa."

He paused and Susa stared at him then smiled and said, "I'll have to thank Tony because only for the accident I wouldn't have known the truth, and at long last I can get rid of you!"

He became very irritated with that remark and shouted, "There's more, and you're not going to like this."

"Go on then, you're dying to tell me so you might as well, before you die!" she replied, waiting for his last attempt to try and humiliate her. And what a blow she was about to get!

"You believed it all, didn't you? All the lies even the one about Owen's accident." Susa's heart missed a beat. What was he talking about she thought, not wanting to show any emotion. He went on but breathing heavily. "You just don't know anyone, Susa, do you? And you wanted to become Mrs Ray Whitfield. You thought he was your friend all these years, didn't you? So why don't you ask him what really happened that day?" He was fading but still trying with every breath to finish his assignment. "Was it a tragic accident with Ray the hero trying to save him? Or did Ray the rapist drown him? I think you'll find the latter to be right Sus-ann-ah!" He started to fade, "Sus-ann-ah you let Owen die. Sus- ann- aaaaa!"

He was gone. Susa stood, frozen, unable to move after that harrowing message. Ray drowning Owen suddenly made sense. That very thought would have made her feel ashamed, but she did think it, she recalled, all those years ago but had immediately blocked it, feeling guilty for allowing herself to believe it. But now she felt it was true. Her heart was pounding. Was this all her fault? That very question was answered instantly as the room lit up, the door opened, and Patrick walked in. He walked slowly over to the settee and lifted the blanket that was over young Susa, then he sat down and held it tightly to his face, weeping uncontrollably. Without knowing he had a witness, he sobbed, "My Susannah. I love you so much. None of this was ever your fault my darling." Susa watched helplessly.

Fifteen

Two weeks went by with Susa still in a coma. Ben, Amy and Ray continued to do their shift patterns faithfully by her side, but now Tony was doing his share too, much to the annoyance of Ray. Tony had been staying with Ben and Amy getting to know them and the kids. Ray of course had raised his concerns over this family reunion and tried very hard to break it up. Dr Carter had alerted them to the reality that Susa may not ever recover and much as they tried to stay positive, as time went on, things did not look good.

Tony arrived to take over from Ben to let him get home for a while. "Don't worry," he said, "I'll call the nurse immediately if she moves. She'll be confused enough without waking up and seeing a stranger sitting next to her."

Tony also told them he needed to go back to Florida very soon as Patrick's health was deteriorating, and he needed him there. "Awe man," he said, "I don't want to leave but I have to. It's been so good of you to put me up. I still can't help feeling this all could have been so different. Was this meant to be? If it was, I need to see the purpose in it. Maybe it's meeting you, buddy."

Just as Ben was about to reply, his mobile rang. "It's Ray," he said unenthusiastically. "Hi, Ray… It's OK, Tony's here now and Amy's coming over… No really, it's OK!… Right bye." He shook his head in frustration.

"What's that guy's problem?" asked Tony.

"I can't take much more of him trying to take control!" said Ben. "It's like he thinks I've to report back to him on everything. Who does he think he is?"

"He is a bit creepy, just sayin', but he's your mum's friend and I suppose you gotta respect that," said Tony, trying to make light of a strange situation.

Just then they heard a slight groan. It was Susa!

"Mum!" cried Ben.

"I'm going to be alright," she said, trying very hard to speak. "Keep Ray away, Ben."

Ben looked at Tony, astounded by this statement. "Take it easy Mum, you've been through a lot."

"Keep Ray away. Bad man. Promise me!"

"I promise you, Mum. But why?"

"I'll tell you soon," she murmured, drifting back into sleep.

Ben called the nurse, then Dr Carter arrived, and they left while he examined her.

Ben and Tony went down to the canteen and Ben rang Amy updating her with the news. They were all astounded at what Susa had said.

"Amy seems to think she probably doesn't know what she's saying at the moment, but I told her she sounded pretty sure and made me promise."

Tony munched his way through a chicken salad sandwich. "He told me the first time I met him that he and your mum were engaged, and it would be better if I went back to America and left her alone, considering I was the one who nearly killed her. That's what he said, man."

"What?" Ben was beginning to understand the dark side of Ray.

"Yeah, my dad never liked him. He made sure he wouldn't make it big in theatre." He wiped the mayo from his face with a serviette and continued, "He never gave me any reason why though, and I didn't ask. I suppose it's because we didn't expect he'd still be hanging around Susannah."

This was like a jigsaw puzzle coming together but with some pieces still missing. "We won't know until Mum's better, but I have a funny feeling there's something bigger that we should know on its way."

Tony nodded in agreement.

"But here's the big question; how are we going to stop Ray from seeing Mum?"

Sixteen

The nurse had Susa sitting up in the bed, but she was still very weak and had fallen asleep. The monitors and all the medical machinery had been taken away and Dr Carter was very happy with her progress. The room seemed brighter, filled with cards and flowers from friends, colleagues and people who remembered her from the theatre. She was a local celebrity with her acting career and participated regularly in raising money for charities, particularly for underprivileged kids to have career opportunities in the theatre. They reported her accident in the local news, but thankfully for her at the moment they know nothing of Tony.

Dr Carter explained to Ben and Tony that Susa was out of danger and would shortly be moved from that ward.

"Great news, doctor," said a delighted Ben. "My mum has come through a lot in her life. She's a survivor. I knew she'd come through this!"

"I knew your father, Ben. We were both students at The General together. He was a great doctor and a good friend. We kept in touch for a while, but life took us on different paths, and we lost touch. I was shocked to hear of his death. He was too young. He had everything to live for," he said shaking his head.

"Thanks, Doctor. I know Dad would have been glad you were here for Mum. We'd better go in and see her now. I don't like leaving her on her own."

"Oh, she's not on her own," replied Doctor Carter. "Ray just arrived when I was leaving."

Tony and Ben looked at one another in horror and quickly made their way to Susa's room, but when they got there Susa was asleep and on her own.

"Where is he?" said a panicky Ben.

"I think we should close the door now in case he comes back," said Tony, desperately trying to figure out a way to keep him out for good.

"OK, but he can still open it and walk in," replied Ben.

Just then, Susa woke up. "Ben! I'm so glad to see you."

Ben was overwhelmed. There were so many things he wanted to say but couldn't. "You've been very sick, Mum, but you're recovering very well. The doctor is very pleased with you," he said and kissed her.

It was a very emotional moment and he looked over at Tony who had stayed in the corner not wanting to scare her. He had tears in his eyes as he watched this reunion.

"I've been on a journey back in my life. Everything's a lie, Ben, and I need you to help. Ray raped me when I was young and he also-" she stopped and began to cry.

"What?" pleaded Ben, trying to hold back his emotions.

"Don't let him near me, please Ben. Patrick Arden is my father." Susa was becoming breathless and unsettled.

"I know, Mum, I know. Now rest."

Susa fell back to sleep. That outburst had taken a lot out of her and left Ben and Tony stunned.

"Could this be true? Not a dream or something?" asked Ben.

"Well, she knew about Dad. That makes me think it's true, and the fact that Ray's a creep! What do you want to do, Ben?" Ben didn't reply, but his body language said everything. "We need to be careful, Ben. We need to keep him away but don't tell him what Susa has said, because if it's true, and I believe it is, we gotta bide our time." These were wise words from Tony, but it was going to be difficult.

Just then, the door opened and in walked Ray with a cup of coffee in his hand. "It's great news, Ben. Your mum's made it. I just popped out to get a coffee; if I had known I would have got you one," he said and went to sit down.

Ben stared at him trying very hard not to punch him but then Tony butted in.

"Yes, I would like a coffee, seeing you're asking," he said in an authoritative tone. Ray looked surprised. "White no sugar."

"Oh, OK," replied Ray, setting his cup down and going back out.

Ben breathed a sigh of relief. "Good thinking, Tony but what now?"

"I'm going to ask him nicely to give you and Amy a few days on your own with your mum," replied Tony.

"There's no way he's going to buy that. He'll know something's up. No, there's no other way than to tell him what Mum has said, and until he's proven innocent, or she says it was a bad dream while in the coma, he can't be allowed anywhere near her."

There wasn't anything else they could do as they had so little time. Ben waited in the corridor and then spotted Ray coming toward him like he was in a hurry, holding tight to the cardboard cup. Ben stopped him in his tracks before he reached the doorway. Tony stood listening where Ray couldn't see him. He heard him professing how shocked he was at this accusation, making himself out to be the victim of a conspiracy and blaming Tony. Yet, after a few moments of confrontation, he left very quickly.

"Easier than I thought," said Ben, surprised.

Amy arrived and passed Ray in the corridor. He turned to her and said,

"I suppose you're part of this ridiculous charade as well?" and walked on.

Amy quickened her step towards Ben. "So, you've told him the news then? I'm sure that wasn't pleasant for you."

"It wasn't pleasant but I'm relieved that Mum was sound asleep."

"What are we going to do? Maybe we should tell the police?"

"No, there's no evidence and you know they'll say she was in a coma."

Tony interrupted, "There you are, he's proved he's guilty. Wouldn't he know that there's no evidence? Yet he went running outta here very quickly when he was confronted. What does that say?"

"You're right, Tony, he is guilty," said Amy. "Remember, Ben, I told you about Susa telling me about 'her ordeal' the morning of the accident?"

"Yes. We'll see what else Mum says. I think there's more but it's not the right time to start asking questions.

Ray's gone now anyway. He'll be too ashamed to come back. But I wonder what else Mum was going to say?"

They went back into the room and found Susa awake. The nurse had been in and got her nice and comfortable in the chair. Tony chose to stay outside until he'd been properly introduced. Ben gave his mum an overview of what had just taken place while Amy stayed beside her, delighted that she was sitting up. She put her hand over Susa's hand and Susa grasped it.

"Susa! How wonderful," said Amy, eager to talk with her.

"Amy, everybody lied to me. Peter tried to tell me that's why he was killed!" Susa was trying so hard to alert them and explain as best she could the things she had uncovered about her life, but it was muddled.

"Susa, you need to slow down. You're safe now. Ray has gone and won't be back. Here take some water and tell us slowly." Amy gave her water and held her hand while Susa began to tell her shortened version. She talked until she was exhausted. Amy felt it was time to introduce her to her brother. An overawed Tony came over to her bedside with Ben.

"Mum this is your brother, Anthony."

Susa's eyes filled with tears. "Anthony. My brother Anthony! I was talking to our dad." They all looked at one another still in awe of her time travel. "You live in Florida. You were in the other vehicle, weren't you?"

No one wanted her to know that Tony was driving the car until she was well enough.

"There's no way she could have known this!" Amy whispered.

"I'm so sorry, Susannah. The brakes failed but how did you know that?"

"It's alright, Anthony. I know everything now."

Seventeen

After Susa had been in hospital for six weeks, they moved her to a bright, light and airy room in the new extension. Nobody had seen or heard from Ray. The atmosphere was so much more positive. Ben, Amy and the children were regular visitors, with Charley wooing all the nurses with his innocent charm. Tony sadly had to travel back to the States to be with Patrick but promised he was going to try very hard to reunite Susa with Patrick before his imminent death. Susa longed for this reunion so much; meeting Patrick would be the healing balm that was needed at this time.

There were many cards, letters and emails she received from people wishing her a speedy recovery. She thought it was time to reply even if it was just to keep her mind occupied from all the bizarre things that had been revealed to her.

It was a day she had looked forward to because Lucinda was coming to visit. Their friendship had seemed to drift apart after Owen's death. It had never been something that she'd questioned because people change and Owen's death had certainly changed her, and Lu had her own little family to contend with. Nonetheless, this now seemed strange, and she needed answers. It had been raining outside but the sun was beginning to burst through the greyish clouds. Susa stopped writing, lay her head back on the pillow and looked around the room. "Everything looks so different now," she said. "Nothing can ever be as it was." She didn't want to cry again. Her tears seemed to be a permanent occurrence. She didn't realise you could get so tired of crying, then she recalled a verse from Psalms that Aunt Martha would say to her on the many occasions when her emotions got the best of her. "Weeping may endure for a night but joy cometh in the morning." That gave her comfort and without thinking she shouted, "Joy comes in the morning!" as if this could push back the tears with her outburst. It worked and she began to laugh and laugh until the door opened and in walked Lu.

"What on earth are you laughing at?" asked a very surprised Lucinda.

"Oh, Lu, it's all mad. Everything's mad," she replied, sounding slightly hysterical.

"Well, you calm down and tell me about all this madness," she said, dashing over to the bed and they hugged for a few moments. "It's so good to see you, Susa. I thought I'd never see you again once I saw the wreckage of your car on the news."

Susa got up from the bed, put her dressing gown on and sat on the chair.

"You look great!" said Lu. "I honestly didn't expect to see you looking so well."

"Thank you," replied Susa who had calmed down and was ready for business. "I really needed to see you, Lu. You have answers to some questions I have about my life. I want you to answer them truthfully as I'm so fed up with lies. Everyone's lied to me."

Lu looked shocked and scared at the same time. "I've never lied to you Susa."

"You knew Bob Henry wasn't my father, didn't you?"

Lu took a step back and stared at Susa, "I didn't know."

"Yes, you did! You did know!"

Lu sat down on the bed and paused the conversation then said quietly, "I didn't know for sure until after Bob passed away, Susa. That's the truth. My mum told me, but I promised her I would never tell you. I'm sorry, I realise now that was an awful thing to do." You could hear by her voice Lucinda becoming emotional.

"It was a cruel and selfish thing to do," said Susa. "I would never have done that to you. I thought our friendship was better than that. I was wrong." It was obvious to Susa that Lu was feeling uncomfortable, but she was just warming up. "You knew Patrick Arden was my father, didn't you?"

Lu stood to her feet. "What?"

"You heard me," replied Susa angrily.

"I didn't know, honestly!" she replied, beginning to pace up and down the room.

"Go on, you're holding something back. Tell me!" demanded Susa.

"Alright, I'm going to, but I need you to know I'm telling you the truth!"

"OK," replied a tamer Susa. "Go on."

Lu stopped pacing and looked at her. "I had heard Mum and Dad talking. This was after she'd told me about Bob not being your dad. I was going to meet with you and Owen for lunch before I headed back to Uni. It was around the time you just got engaged. I was about to go into the kitchen to ask Dad for a lift, but something stopped me. Dad said to Mum, "I wonder will her real dad come forward and walk her down the aisle?" And Mum answered, "He's too busy writing his plays but keeps a close eye on her from afar."

I didn't really understand what she meant by that until that awful night at his house and I saw how concerned he was for you. I couldn't tell you because I didn't know for sure and you appeared to be so happy with Owen and getting married, and with your work. Your life was good."

"It was a lie!" Susa shouted. "A big, fat, ugly lie! And you knew it!"

Lucinda was visibly upset. "I'm going to go, Susa. This is not helping you at all and I want you better. I know you're angry and I understand. If I could change the past now I would. I can only say how sorry I am."

Tears were in her eyes and Susa knew she was genuinely sorry. "I don't want you to go. I forgive you, Lu. I had forgiven you even before you came here today. Now, I need to ask you about Ray."

"Ray?"

"Yes, what you thought of him. Did you like him? Did you trust him?"

Lu looked horrified. "Oh, my goodness. That's a strange question but I said I'd tell you the truth and I will. I couldn't stand him. Chip didn't like him either. We all tolerated him for your sake, and as for trust, no way! He was always trying to be the centre of attention, pretending he was the most popular person on earth, always making horrible comments about Chip."

Susa looked in shock. "How could I have been so stupid, Lu?"

Lu hugged her. "You were never stupid, Susa, vulnerable sometimes yes, but never stupid."

"He raped me! It was Ray who raped me!"

Lu released her arms from around Susa and stared at her. "What? Ray! That's sick! I can't imagine how you feel. How did you find all this out?" asked a stunned Lu, quite speechless but drinking in all this emerging news.

Susa went on to tell her about her time travel experiences.

"I've never heard of such a thing in my life! It's all so accurate, and Tony, that's just, wow!" declared Lu.

"I know, I can't get it all out of my head. There's so much I'm really struggling with, but I have to know everything now."

"Of course," agreed Lu.

"There's one more thing I need to know, why did our friendship decline when Owen died? I rarely saw you after that and I needed you so much."

Lucinda shook her head in despair. "You mean you don't know?"

"No! What?" said Susa, looking fearful of what was about to be said.

"Ray, that's why." Lu kept on shaking her head.

"What did he do?"

"He told me that you told him you needed me to back off, that you needed time on your own with Ben to grieve and that he would let me know when the time was right. I'm sure you know by now he didn't get back to me. That's why; I thought you didn't want me anymore; I was so hurt.

I should have known he was a liar, but he was so convincing when he told me. I feel such a fool now," Lu sobbed.

"Right, now I understand. Then it won't surprise you if I told you that I have reason to believe - but can't prove - that he wasn't trying to save Owen from drowning, he drowned him!"

Lu stopped sobbing and stared at her in disbelief. "What?"

"Yes, he did Lu. I know that now and I know it in here," she said pointing to her heart.

"You need to get the police involved, Susa. I'm really concerned for you, especially now that he knows he's been found out. You know what a rat does once it's cornered. He's obviously been obsessed with you all along like you're his property and nobody else can have you. Patrick was right, he's a creep but a very dangerous one."

Susa knew Lucinda was right but what was she going to do?

Eighteen

"You'll never guess who's here, Mum," said a very excited Ben.

"Who?" replied Susa.

"Uncle Tony!" shouted Martha.

"Really? He's back already, but I thought he needed to be with Patrick?"

Tony walked through the door with a bouquet of red roses and set them on her knee. "These are from Dad. He sent me here to bring you back to Florida with me. He's a little stronger since he heard you wanted to see him. It's like a new lease of life. Your ticket is booked, and I've spoken with Dr Carter. He said Florida is exactly what you need."

Susa laughed, "This is wonderful but when? I need to get out of here first."

"You are getting out of here tomorrow and going to Florida with me, the next day, big sister."

Susa was overjoyed with this news. "I can't wait to see him!"

Unknown to the happy family, they were being watched by Ray. He had been keeping guard very quietly for a few days now, sometimes incognito, like a jackal waiting for his moment to pounce.

"OK, I have a lot to do now so that I can get out of here tomorrow. Ben, I need you to take those bags home with you and Tony you take the suitcase."

Martha ran around the room so excited that Grandma was better, and she could have her back again all to herself very soon.

"Kisses please!" said Susa, and Martha reacted immediately with arms outstretched.

Then they left her to pack, thrilled that this nightmare had at long last come to an end. Or had it?

Susa looked at the beautiful bouquet and got a vase from the cabinet under the sink, but before she could fill it with water, she felt a shiver run down her spine, as she heard the voice of the one person she never wanted to see again.

"So, you think that it's over between you and me?" She turned to see Ray at the door. "Just because that jerk Tony tells you lies, and you believe him doesn't mean it's over." He closed the door behind him, walked over to the window on the other side of the room and turned to face a very frightened Susa.

She managed to speak with a little confidence in her voice, "What are you doing here, Ray? You're not welcome."

"Oh, but I am. Remember you and I are going to get married. I need you Susa, you know that, and you've always known that. I've done everything for you, and this is the thanks I get. I don't think so!" He walked slowly over to her as she stared at him, wondering how she could protect herself. "All those years of my life I gave to you, and you never cared. Making me a laughing stock with all your so-called friends." She couldn't think why she had never seen this disturbing side of him.

"Awe man! I forgot Susannah's suitcase," Tony said just as he was about to get into the car. "I'll go back and get it. I won't be long."

He marched quickly across the car park, through the automatic glass doors and into the elevator. As he stepped out, he bumped into Dr Carter.

"Oh, hi Doctor. I forgot Susa's suitcase. She wanted us all out of the way so she could get everything sorted for leaving in the morning," he said looking flustered.

"Oh, then you better take Ray as well!" he laughed.

"Why do you say that?" he asked, hoping he had heard him wrong.

"Because he's there with Susannah now," he replied looking confused at Tony's reaction.

"Quickly, phone the police. It's urgent, doctor. Fast! He's dangerous!"

Tony ran down the corridor leaving a bewildered but obedient Dr Carter running behind talking on his mobile.

"Owen was never right for you. He didn't know you the way I did," continued Ray, moving closer to Susa. She kept her eyes pinned to his, to keep control, praying for help. "You're mine, Susa, and no one will take you away from me. You need me too."

He seized the bouquet and threw it on the floor still staring at Susa, not realising a thorn from a rose had stuck in his finger. He stood so close to her that she could smell the stale alcohol lingering on his breath.

"You remember how good it was between us. You remember that night very well, don't you?" he said in a deep, low voice while putting his hand up to her face and stroking her cheek.

She felt sick, but then he saw the blood coming from his finger and it distracted him. He took his eyes off Susa, pulling his hand from her face. This split second gave her the opportunity to defend herself, and before he knew it, she had smashed the vase over his head. He fell to the floor, staring at her with such venom and with blood flowing down his face.

"You bitch. You dirty ungrateful bitch!"

The door opened, and Tony and Dr Carter ran in as Susa screamed hysterically, "You drugged me and raped me you snake!"

"You wanted it!" shouted Ray. "You were crying out for it!" forgetting about the two witnesses now present.

"And you killed Owen!"

"Yes, and I'm glad. I hated him. I'm glad he's dead."

Susa stood rooted to the spot.

"That's enough Ray!" shouted Tony. "You can tell all this to the police; they're on their way."

The security guards ran in and handcuffed Ray and within minutes the police arrived.

Nineteen

Susa lay back in bed, with Ben, Amy and Tony faithfully by her side.

"He's gone now, Susa. You won't have to look at him again. You must be exhausted. You've come through so much," said Amy.

Susa stared out the window certainly not with the enthusiasm she had earlier that morning when they announced the ticket to Florida. "I'm so tired," she said, trying very hard to talk.

"Come on, Amy, we'll go and let her sleep. It's been a chaotic day," said Ben, going over to Susa and kissing her on the cheek. "We'll see you in the morning, Mum. I can't wait for you to come home. Sleep now, you've a busy day tomorrow."

Susa gently stroked his face, "I love you, darling," she said as she fell asleep.

"At last, she looks so peaceful now," said Tony.

They all kissed a very tranquil Susa goodnight before they went, appreciating this last night at the hospital.

There was not a sound. You could hear a pin drop. Susa was in a deep sleep but stirred as she felt a warm, tender touch on her hand. It felt safe. It happened again only this time she comfortably clasped it as if it was the most natural thing to do. It was like a dream. She began to wake knowing there was a strong presence in the room with her and feeling a calm sensation beside her. She opened her eyes to see who was there.

"What are you doing here?" she smiled at Patrick.

"I have to go now, Susannah," he said. "But I need to tell you how sorry I am for not being there for you. It's the biggest regret of my life but I love you. I'm so proud of you and everything you've achieved." He looked old and tired.

"You're leaving now?" asked Susa, understanding this dreamlike situation. "Yes, but I want to give you this." In his other hand was a ring. "That was for your mother. I want you to keep it."

"Thank you," she said. "But please don't go! Life can never be the same again."

Twenty

The next morning excitement filled the air in the Spence household. Charlie and Martha had their own personal art covering a designated wall in Susa's room. Amy was doing some last-minute tidying. There was a more sombre atmosphere in the kitchen where Tony was having coffee with Ben.

"He murdered my dad, Tony. How do you get over something like this?"

"You can't, Ben. It's gonna take time."

Ben stared out the window and sipped his coffee. "I hope they throw away the key. How's Mum ever going to cope with all this?"

"Come on now. He's not going to ruin this day for us. You finally get your mum back, and don't worry she's gonna have the best care in Florida." Tony was feeling a little nostalgic. "It's been quite a journey these last few months meeting ya'll this way, the family I never knew I had. I just wish Dad would have told me years ago. I could have been there for you, Ben. Ray wouldn't have been in your lives that's for sure! I would've seen through that shmuk alright. Susannah's a wonderful lady. I know she and I will be great friends even at this later stage, but I can't help feeling it's all so damn sad," he said, shaking his head in sorrow.

Ben looked at him affectionately. "It's done now and there's nothing any of us can do about that. We can't change what's happened. Mum had come to terms with everything, and she was happy, especially since the kids were born. It was just that murdering scum! He always had to be in control, but Mum could never see it. Now I know why I detested him. I even felt guilty for that because he'd been there when Mum needed him."

Tony grunted something looking like he was in deep thought, before saying, "He really loved your grandma, you know. I mean my dad. He said she was the love of his life and that it was the happiest time he ever had. When he heard Bob Spence had died, he wanted to see Elsie again. He didn't know she had left him after Peter's accident. Sadly, it was too late when he went to find her. Elsie had passed away the year previous. He was gutted, man! He even had a ring made for her, nine-carat gold with their names engraved on the inside. He never got to give it to her. He kept it in the drawer beside his bed. What a love story that wasn't meant to be."

Just then Amy disrupted their bonding moment, "Right you two, you need to go and get Susa. You know what she's like in the morning. She'll have had her breakfast and will have everything organised and waiting on you."

"Even at this time?" asked a surprised Tony.

"Especially at this time," she laughed.

At 8 a.m. Tony and Ben had just arrived at the hospital. They were both now more upbeat and feeling there was a new beginning in their lives.

"I'm definitely going to write a book about this someday, buddy," said Tony as they entered the elevator.

"No one would believe it!" laughed Ben.

The elevator doors opened, and they strolled down the corridor, happily knowing this would be the last time they would visit this place. It would now just be a memory, bad, sad and happy!

They could see two nurses standing outside Susa's room. One of them called to Dr Carter who immediately marched up the corridor to meet them. He didn't look happy.

"What's going on?" asked a concerned Ben.

"I'm so sorry to be the bearer of bad news," said Dr Carter shaking his head.

"Ah, no, don't tell me she can't be discharged today?" replied Ben.

"I'm sorry Ben, it's worse than that I'm afraid."

"What then?" he asked cautiously.

"Your mother has passed away. I'm so sorry. At the moment we can only tell you that she died between 5 and 6 a.m. this morning. It was her heart."

Stunned, Ben and Tony stood there, speechless and bewildered.

"I can't believe this," said Tony.

"This can't be happening," said Ben.

"You may of course go and see her. If there's anything I can do, please let me know." He walked off leaving Tony and Ben almost dazed.

They looked at her lifeless body. "It's like she's sleeping, but she's not," said Ben. "How could this have happened?"

The nurse knocked on the door politely. "Could I speak with you for a moment?"

"Yes, of course," replied Ben.

"It's just I have something that was in your mother's hand when she died." She went over to the drawer beside her bed, took out a ring and handed it to Ben. "I'm sure she would want you to have it." He looked curiously at the ring. "Tony, did you say 9-carat gold with their names engraved?"

"Why, yes," he replied.

"Well, that's the ring."

"No way, man!"

They sat, completely dumbfounded for a few minutes until Tony's mobile rang. "What?" he said. "That's not possible, he can't have. He was doing so well. At what time? I'll have to ring you back, Susannah has just died as well." He ended the call. "That was Dad's nurse. He's dead!"

"No!"

"But that's not all; he died at the same time as Susannah."

There was silence, then Ben lifted the ring in full view of both of them. "Tony, are you thinking what I'm thinking?"

"Yes," he said, smiling, "I am thinking what you're thinking!"

Available worldwide from Amazon
and all good bookstores

Michael Terence
Publishing

www.mtp.agency

mtp.agency

@mtp_agency

Made in the USA
Columbia, SC
25 November 2024

47248000R00062